The Song of
Igor's Campaign

D0872876

The Song of Igor's Campaign

Translated, with a Foreword by
Vladimir Nabokov

ARDIS PUBLISHERS
WOODSTOCK & NEW YORK

This edition first published in the United States in 2003 by
Ardis Publishers
Woodstock & New York

WOODSTOCK:
One Overlook Drive
Woodstock, NY 12498
[for individual orders, bulk and special sales, contact our Woodstock office]

NEW YORK:
141 Wooster Street
New York, NY 10012

Ardis Publishers is an imprint of Peter Mayer Publishers, Inc.
www.ardisbooks.com

Cataloging-in-Publication Data is available from the Library of Congress

Printed in Canada
ISBN 0-87501-061-X
1 3 5 7 9 8 6 4 2

The Song of
Igor's Campaign

FOREWORD

1

According to the annals[1] of Kievan Russia, four territorial princes with throne towns on the rivers Desna and Seim, east of Chernigov, set out on Tuesday, April 23, 1185, for the prairies beyond the river Donets to fight the Kumans. The four princes were: Igor,[2] leader of the expedition; his brother, Vsevolod;[3] their nephew, Svyatoslav;[4] and Igor's young son, Vladimir.[5] The Kumans,[6] nomads of obscure Turco-Mongolian origin, who had been assailing the southeastern steppes for the last hundred years, had been soundly trounced in 1183 by Igor's cousin, Svyatoslav III.[7] Igor was moved by the spirit of rash emulation in undertaking his own expedition without consulting the senior prince.

Igor's mounted troops, marching leisurely in a general southeasterly direction, took nine days to cover the distance, about 250 miles, between Igor's throne town, Novgorod-Seversk, and the river Donets. They continued southward, through oak brush and pine barren, between the Donets and the Oskol. In the steppes some 80 miles south of the junction of those two rivers, about 400 miles from Novgorod-Seversk, they clashed with the Kumans. On Sunday, May 12, after three days of fighting, the army of the four princes was completely defeated. They were captured by four different khans[8] and taken to four different camps. In the course of the following months the Kumans invaded Russian territory between the Sula and Seim rivers and retreated with a rich booty.

After at least one year of captivity Igor managed to escape. In the meantime young Vladimir, in *his* place of confinement, married the daughter of Khan Konchak. Vladimir was back in Russia, with wife and child, by the autumn of 1187, and it is reasonable to suppose that his uncle, Vsevolod, had also been liberated by that time. The fourth member of the expedition apparently died in captivity.

Six centuries later, around 1790, Count Aleksey Musin-Pushkin, collector of antiquities and high-ranking lay member of the Synod, had the singular good fortune to acquire a certain batch of old manuscripts. His agent (whose name was never divulged) bought them—so the count asserted in 1813—from the archimandrite Joel (*Ioil'*), "a man of culture and a lover of literature": he had administered the Spaso-Yaroslavskiy monastery till 1788, at which time it was turned into an *arhiereyskiy dom* ("episcopal house"). Upon the dissolution of the monastery, Joel had lapsed into indigence and was glad to have Musin's mysterious commissioner buy from him the manuscripts that had belonged to the disbanded cloister. Among these was a magnificent literary masterpiece, half poem, half oration, henceforth to be known as the *Slóvo o polkú Ígoreve*,[9] The Song of Igor's Campaign. It was bound, with several other manuscripts, in a volume marked "Nr. 323" where it was placed fifth.[10] Its text presented a mass of more or less fused, often abbreviated or not completed words "on glossy paper . . . in a rather neat hand." [11] A modicum of internal evidence, which most scholars today believe to be not an injection by a Russian Macpherson, but a natural exhalation of inherent truth, forces one to assume that the unknown author of the song composed it in the spring or early summer of 1187.[12] The actual text discovered by Musin was, however, a much later transcript made, it is conjectured, in the sixteenth century, and not in Kiev but perhaps in Pskov, by a monastic scribe who could not understand a number of old words and phrases which consequently he botched.[13] In preparing the First Edition, Musin and his two coeditors (Bantïsh-Kamenski, director of the Archives in Moscow, and his assistant, Malinovski) separated the words (sometimes incorrectly), introduced modern punctuation and rather haphazardly paragraphed the text.[14] They also printed *en regard* a modern Russian version which abounds in all kinds of inaccuracies, pseudoclassical paraphrases, and glaring blunders. This First Edition of the *Slovo o polku Igorevye, Igorya sïna Svyatoslavlya, vnuka Ol'gova* (The Song of the Campaign of Igor, Igor Son of Svyatoslav [and] Grandson of Oleg) came out in Moscow on December 5, 1800, in a volume entitled *Iroicheskaya pyesn' | o | pohodye na polovtsov | udyel'nago knyazya Novagoroda-Syeverskago | Igorya Svyatoslavicha, | pisannaya | starinnïm russkim yazïkom | v iskhodye XII stolyetiya | s perelozheniem na upotreblyaemoe nïnye naryechie. | Moskva | v Senatskoy Tipografii, | 1800.* (The heroic song of the campaign against the Kumans of the territorial prince [*udel*-owner, "independent prince"] of Novgorod-Seversk, Igor son of Svyatoslav, written in the ancient Russian language at the close of the twelfth century, with a transposition into the idiom now in use).[15]

The precious manuscript of the *Slovo* perished during the Moscow conflagration of 1812 when Musin's house was burned to the ground. All we possess in the way of basic material is the edition of 1800 and an apograph that in 1795 or 1796 Count Musin-Pushkin had a scribe make from the MS for Empress Catherine II. This Apograph (known as the *Arhivnïy*, or *Ekaterininskiy, Spisok*), which differs only in a few insignificant details from the *editio princeps*, was discovered among Catherine's papers more than six decades later by the historian Pekarski, who published it in 1864 in an Appendix 2 to volume V, 1862, of *Zapiski Imperatorskoy Akademii Nauk* (Memoirs of the Imperial Academy of Sciences).

It was during the preparation of the Apograph and of three or four additional copies (now lost) that the news of Musin's remarkable acquisition spread among the lovers of Russian letters. They learned that not only had a great bard flourished in Russia at the end of the twelfth century but that he had had a predecessor named Boyan[16] in the eleventh. Of the author of The Song, we do not know the name but know the work; of his predecessor, we do not know the name but possess only such samples of his work as are alluded to in The Song.

2

The original text of The Song as published in 1800 consists of 14,175 letters or about 2850 words. I have divided it, in my English literal translation, into 860 lines. Its first sections are devoted mainly to an account of the unfortunate foray. The facts tally with those of the Ipatiev Chronicle but they are grouped and illumined according to the poet's own views and needs. That there was some exchange of information between the original chronicler and the author of The Song is evident from a few bizarre coincidences (see for example notes to lines 91 and 814-830), but who was influenced by whom is far from clear. The chronicle is the work of a learned monk adept at pious formulas, a conscientious writer with a shapeless style and little originality of thought. The Song, on the other hand, is a harmonious, many leveled, many hued, uniquely poetical structure created in a sustained and controlled surge of inspiration by an artist with a fondness for pagan gods and a percipience of sensuous things. Its political and patriotic slant pertaining to a given historical moment is, naturally, of small importance in the light of its timeless beauty, and although I have provided the reader with all necessary notes, I am not interested in considering The Song as a corollary of history or a birch-stump speech.

The structure of The Song shows a subtle balance of parts which attests to deliberate artistic endeavor and excludes the possibility of that gradual accretion of lumpy parts which is so typical of folklore. It is the lucid work of one man, not the random thrum of a people. From the extraordinary prelude, where the tenacious shadow of Boyan is used by our bard for his own narrative purpose, to the conclusion of the work, where Boyan is once more invoked to preside over the happy end, there is a constant interplay of themes and mutual echoes. The entire composition neatly divides itself into five parts: 1. Exordium (lines 1-70); 2. Narration (lines 71-390); 3. Conjuration (391-730); 4. Liberation (lines 731-830); 5. Epilogue (lines 831-860). In Part 2, Vsevolod's speech to his brother before they set out (lines 71-90) forms a companion piece to the description of Vsevolod in action on the battlefield (lines 211-230); the bright sun which is eclipsed in 91-110, when Igor addresses his warriors before the campaign, later rises in gory grandeur over the battlefield (181-183), is addressed by Euphrosyne from the rampart (722-730), and finally sheds a gay and benevolent radiance on Igor's homecoming (841). In another ingenious arrangement of nicely fitting pieces, the Winds, which in Part 2 drive enemy arrows against Igor (197-199), are conjured by Euphrosyne in Part 3 (699-708), and in answer to her prayer brew up a diversionary storm (731-732) to assist Igor's liberation. Especially satisfying to one's sense of inner concord and unity is the ample treatment of the theme of the Rivers, among which the Great Don plays a leading role. Igor's urge to take a look at it (100) and drink a helmetful of it (110), expressed in a stylistically perfect refrain at the beginning of Part 1, is repeated with a symmetrical intonation at 180 and 190, in the beginning of the great battle, when the resounding, redoubtable Don is felt to be on the side of the Kumans. Throughout The Song that river is mentioned a number of times in terms of terror and disaster (131, 194, 205, 309, 741) as well as in terms of passionate desire (100, 110, 416, 503, 567), with the subtheme of the "helmetful" repeated at 416 and 503. Igor does not attain the blue mirage of the Don (which will be reached two centuries later in the *Zadonshchina*, a vulgar imitation of The Song concocted in celebration of a great victory over the Mongols), but in a perfect structural move the artist substitutes for the Great Don its tributary, the Lesser Don, the "little" Donets, with which, or rather with whom, the prince in the Liberation part of The Song indulges in a charming colloquy (771-802), contrasting the kind Donets with a much less amiable stream, the Stugna, in a passage (791-802) which resolves itself in a last echo of danger and misfortune. Igor's speech of thanks to the Lesser Don is beautifully duplicated by his wife's prayer to the Dnepr (711-719): the great Kievan river transmits as it were the power of intercession and assistance to the prairie stream, and Igor's historical recollection of a less fortunate lady's weeping on the Dnepr's banks is a necessary element of rhetorical harmony to balance, at the close of the entire movement, Euphrosyne's initial apostrophization of that river. And finally there is the river Kayala, near which the disastrous battle is fought. The reiteration of its name with emblematic allusions is a haunting presence throughout The Song (194, 251, 292, 380, 431, 694).

An array of animals, resembling the stylized fauna of rich-hued rugs, and marginal designs of delicate plants play a changeful double role in the structure of The Song. They give its circumstances a touch of local reality, and they participate in the general theme of magic, prophecy and conjuration, a theme bespeaking a singular freedom of thought and distinguishing this pagan poem from the pallid and rigid compositions of routine Christian piety which by that time had begun to direct and to drain literary art. It will be noted that here again the diverse expressions of the theme enter into a subtle arrangement of calls and recalls, with every step having its reverberation and every echo its arch. Thus, the colorful prairie creatures participating as agents of doom and as the Kumans' allies in the excitement of the eclipse (115-126, 132-139) or taking cruel advantage of the dead (263-266, 602-604), or reveling in tragedy (406-407, 422-443), are replaced and responded to, within the work's plural melody, by the antiphonal pro-Russian birds (787-790, 806-813), assistants of the river gods conjured by Euphrosyne and, in the case of the nightingales, representatives of Boyan.

In what may be termed a more feminine strain, flowers and trees by their drooping movements express their choral compassion for the misfortunes of the Russians. Besides an allusion at 562, the formula of their participation occurs as a refrain at 299-301 and again at 801-802: it comes here during that triumphant homeward trek where, seemingly, nothing but elation could be experienced by Igor, but where, by an artistic device, the pathetic refrain lends a poetically needful support to the symmetry of the over-arching theme of melancholy; which melancholy is now transformed into a remembered event referring to a long-dead prince and thus brings out, in vibrant contrast, among the light and shade of riverside willows, the lucky fate of the live hero.

The all-pervading sense of magic so vividly conveyed by flora and fauna, demon peacocks and fairytale ducks, waters and winds, auroras and thunders, is introduced by our bard's descriptions of Boyan's enchantments (especially 11-18 and 35-38) and is further illustrated by a series of thematic panels such as the Eclipse (91-119), the Portentous Storm following it (132-139 and 181-190), the Arrival of the Antivirgin (306-310), the King's Dream (391-410), the Spells of Vseslav (651-690), Euphrosyne's Incantation (691-750) and Igor's Escape (especially 731-733, 751-760, 781-790, 806-810).

Among other elements of our author's technique the good reader will note his art of transition and preparation. Thus, interrupting with a dramatic aside the account of the battle which starts with the "Vsevolod Wild Bull" movement (211-230), our bard, in preparation of the political centerpiece of The Song (that magnificent section, 497-686, where old feuds are recalled and contemporaneous princes implored to help Igor), contrives a first digression beginning at 231, "There have been the ages of Troyan" (which in itself is a companion intonation to the Boyan apostrophe at 51-60), and continuing to 270, after which we return to the Kayala battlefield. In this long digression the feuds of Oleg Malglory (233-238), the death of Boris son of Vyacheslav (245-250) and that of Izyaslav I (251-254) are recalled, and the image of a dissension-torn Russia (255-268) is projected from there into another section (311-350) where a clamor of lament rises after Igor's defeat. The transition from that defeat to the recent victories of Svyatoslav III leads to the great scene in Kiev, while the various evocations, pictorial in brightness and dramatic in sonority, of Oleg, Vyacheslav and Izyaslav have now prepared eye and ear for the brilliant glimpses of princes who are rallied to Igor's assistance: Yaroslav of Chernigov (466-478), Vsevolod of Suzdal (497-510), the brothers Rurik and David (511-522), Yaroslav of Galich (523-541), Roman later of Galich and his brother Mstislav (542-559) and Mstislav's brothers Ingvar and Vsevolod (571-582), after which a historical recollection, the recent death of Izyaslav son of Vasilko (591-610), leads to the admirable evocation of the enchantments and misfortunes of Vseslav, Izyaslav's grandfather (631-678).

Within these ample surgings of interlinked themes we can mark such smaller elements of inner unity as intonational refrains and recurrent types of metaphor. Among the refrains are such striking repetitions of euphonious formulas as "seeking for themselves honor and for their prince glory" (89-90, 149-150), "O Russian land, you are already behind the culmen" (140-141, 195-196), the double formula of "drooping" pertaining to grass and trees (299-301), to ramparts and merriment (387-390), to voices and merriment (611-614) and, in perfect structural symmetry, to the flowers and the tree at 801-802. Another refrain is the plea to avenge Russia and Igor (519-523, 539-541, 580-583); and "Yaroslavna early weeps in Putivl on the rampart, repeating" is an especially musical reiteration recalling Western European ballads (697-698, 709-710, 720-721). Finally, I leave to the students of generic style to notice the various categories of metaphor which adorn The Song and add the pleasures of connotation to those of direct imagery. These metaphors can be classified mainly as belonging to the vocabulary of the hunt, to the domain of agriculture and to that of meteorological phenomena.

3

Throughout The Song there occur here and there a few poetical formulas strikingly resembling those in Macpherson's *Ossian*. I discuss them in my Commentary. Paradoxically, these coincidences tend to prove not that a Russian of the eighteenth century emulated Macpherson, but that Macpherson's concoction does contain after all scraps derived from authentic ancient poems. It is not unreasonable to assume that through the mist of Scandinavian sagas certain bridges or ruins of bridges may be distinguished linking Scottic-Gaelic romances with Kievan ones. The curious point is that if we imagine a Russian forger around 1790 constructing a mosaic out of genuine odds and ends with his own mortar, we must further imagine that he knew English well enough to be affected by specific elements of Macpherson's style; but in the eighteenth century, and well into the age of Pushkin, English poetry was known to Russians only through French versions, and therefore the Russian forger would not have rendered, as Letourneur did not render them, the very special details of that curious "Ossianic" style of which I give examples in my notes.

The eleventh and twelfth centuries were marked in Kievan Russia by amazing artistic achievements, but the making of diadems, frescoes, ikons, and marvelously lovely churches, such as the Cathedral of St. Sophia in Kiev (built in 1036) or the Uspenskiy Cathedral in Vladimir (1158-1189) or the Dmitrievskiy Cathedral in the same town (1193-1197), does not necessarily imply a contemporaneous development of literature; and similarly, great poetry is known to have been produced at periods when the (on the whole more primitive) arts of painting and architecture did not exactly flourish. Despite the Marxist scholastics and nationalistic emotions which tend to transform modern essays on The Song into exuberant hymns to the Motherland, Soviet historians are as helpless as earlier Russian scholars were to explain the striking, obvious, almost palpable difference in artistic texture that exists between The Song and such remnants of Kievan literature as have reached us across the ages. Had only those chronicles and sermons, and testaments, and humdrum lives of saints been preserved, the Kievan era would have occupied a very modest nook in the history of medieval European literature; but as things stand, one masterpiece not only lords it over Kievan letters but rivals the greatest European poems of its day.

Considerations of historical perspective prevent one from believing that The Song was composed around 1790 by an anonymous poet endowed with a degree of genius exceeding in originality and force that of the only major poet of the time (Derzhavin) and possessing an amount of special erudition in regard to the Kievan era which none in his time possessed. Suggestions to the effect that a forger gave up a future of personal fame in order to glorify the past of his country, or that he was able to avail himself of documents which are now lost, immediately provoke new questions requiring new conjectures to deal with them. But after all this has been said, and the possibility of fraud contemptuously dismissed, and the entire burden of its proof shifted onto the frail shoulders of insufficient scholarship, we still have to cope with certain eerie doubts.

We are faced by the unnatural combination of two generically different notions: we are forced, first, to assume that at a singularly precise point in historical reality, namely in the early summer of 1187, somewhere in Kievan Russia a person describes—pen in hand or harp in lap—a series of events which started only two years before and are still in a state of live flux and formlessness; and second, we are forced to combine in our mind this political, local, actual, journalistic reality with the impact of such poetical imagery in The Song as is usually associated with the maturity of fondly manipulated impressions and with a long period of time—a decade, a century—elapsing between the event and the metaphor. In other words, it is very difficult to imagine the author of The Song singing the actual dew with which Igor's cloak was still wet as he rode into Kiev, or echoing Euphrosyne's sobs while she was actually rushing down from her wooden tower in Putivl to embrace her prince; or turning into a mannered dialogue the panting messenger's news of Vladimir's bringing home a wife from the Kuman steppe.

4

The existence of The Song in manuscript form at some point of time between the end of the twelfth century and the end of the fourteenth century is attested by there being an imitation of it knocked together at the latter time limit and discovered only in the middle of the last century, six decades after The Song came to light. This is the composition generally known as the *Zadonshchina*.

On the misty morning of September 8, 1380, on the Kulikovo Field, a united Russian army of some 150,000 men, from almost all the existing princedoms, under the leadership of

Prince Dmitri of Moscow (d. 1389) assisted by the princes Andrey of Polotsk, Dmitri of Bryansk, Dmitri of Volïn and Vladimir of Serpuhov, having forded the Don at the mouth of its affluent, the Nepryadva (in the present Tula region), engaged in a tremendous battle with twice as many Tatars led by Khan Mamay, and won Russia's first big victory over the Mongols after a century and a half of servitude. A few years later, probably around 1385 (judging by internal evidence) the Kulikovo Battle was sung and discoursed upon by a certain Sophonias (*Sofon, Sofoniy* or *Sofoniya*), a priest from Ryazan (or perhaps a gentleman from Bryansk turned monk after a military career). This composition has reached us in half a dozen transcripts, none of them good, of which the main ones are entitled:

1. *Zadonshchina* [the Beyond-the-Don Campaign] of the Great Prince Dmitri son of Ivan and his cousin Vladimir son of Andrey, being a manuscript of 1470, discovered in the St. Cyril monastery of Belozersk, and first published in 1859.

2. *Skazaniye* [the Narrative, or Tale] by Sofon the Ryazanian, in praise of the princes Dmitri and Vladimir, a manuscript of the XVII c., in the Library of the Synod, first published in 1890; and

3. *Slovo* [the Song, or Discourse] about the princes Dmitri and Vladimir, a manuscript of the XVII c., published by its discoverer, Undolski, in 1852.

Of these texts, the first is the shortest; its title, *Zadonshchina*, is traditionally used to signify the entire sorry thing as known from the transcripts. Sophonias, an enthusiastic but clumsy plagiarist, adapted the general structure of the first two parts of The Song of Igor's Campaign and a jumble of specific details (epithets, images, rhetorical formulas) to a generalized description of the Kulikovo Battle. Some of the details he did not understand, and his floundering attempts to incorporate them in his imitation led to a preposterous mixture of inchoate bombast, meaningless metaphors, and his own patriotic platitudes. It belongs to the

FOREWORD

coarse and ponderously didactic Moscow era which succeeded the marvelously artistic Kievan one. The *Zadonshchina* differs from The Song of Igor as sackcloth from samite.

Not Boyan, but "the nightingale bird" (St. Cyril text) or "the nightingale, summer bird, joy of fair days" (Synod text), is bluntly and lamely suggested as a singer of the Kulikovo heroes. The mysterious, wonderfully poetical phrase of The Song addressed to the Russian land, *"uzhe za Shelomyanem esi"* (you are already behind the hill), is turned into the ludicrous *"kak esi bila doseleva za tsarem' za Solomonom, tak budi i ninyecha za knyazem' velikim Dmitriem"* of the same St. Cyril text (a phrase which if it means anything at all may be translated as "even now shall you be under Great Prince Dmitri as you were under King Solomon"). The passage of The Song (492-493), "now in Rim [people] scream under Kuman sabers," becomes in the St. Cyril text of the *Zadonshchina*, "the *divo* calls under the Tatar sabers." And Euphrosyne's incantation is distributed among several garrulous ladies.[17]

5

In my translation of The Song I have ruthlessly sacrificed manner to matter and have attempted to give a literal rendering of the text as I understand it.[18] Each page (except the first, the last, and one in the middle) of the lost original contained presumably an average of 310 letters (arranged in about twenty lines of about the same length each). I have preserved on each page of my English translation the amount of material corresponding to what I think was that amount on each given page of the lost MS (or, more correctly, of an earlier MS on which Musin's MS was based); but the breaking up of these batches into lines is arbitrary and only meant to provide easy reference.

No satisfactory edition of The Song exists in Russian. By satisfactory I mean a volume that would include among other things photostats of the First Edition and of the Apograph, a summary of all recensions and commentaries and a complete bibliography. We can light-heartedly go without the "poetical" versions of The Song and articles on its politico-national importance, all of which are so lavishly represented in Soviet editions.

Among recent works the most useful are Lihachyov's commentaries in *Slovo o polku Igoreve*, edited by Miss Adrianov-Peretts, Leningrad, 1950; those by Kudryashov, Eleonski and Rzhiga in *Slovo o polku Igoreve*, edited by Klobukovski and Kuzmin, Moscow, 1947; and Dmitriev's commentaries in his edition of the same work, Leningrad, 1952. Another useful edition is *La Geste du Prince Igor, texte établi, traduit et commenté sous la direction d'* Henri Grégoire, *de* Roman Jakobson *et de* Marc Szeftel *assistés de* J. A. Joffe, New York, 1948. This contains among other matter a poor English version of The Song by Samuel Cross more or less patched up by the editors. I have also seen the *Tale of the Armament of Igor*, edited and translated by Leonard A. Magnus, Oxford, 1915, a bizarre blend of incredible blunders, fantastic emendations, erratic erudition and shrewd guesses. It has some clearly presented genealogical charts. Some of these I have used, revising them in the light of data selected from the other works listed above, in compiling the Pedigree of Princes primed on page 24. When identifying the princes variously involved in The Song, the reader must be prepared to countenance a formidable recurrence of the same syllables. As will be seen from the Index and the Pedigree (where the "great princes" enthroned in Kiev are recognizable by the regal numerals affixed to their names) the termination in *slav* (meaning "glory," "glorious") is most frequent. There are six Svyatoslavs (Sv. I, d. 972; Sv. II, d. 1076; Sv. III, d. 1194; Sv. of Chernigov, Igor's father, d. 1164; Sv. of Rïlsk, Igor's nephew, d. 1186; and Sv., Igor's small son) and six Mstislavs. Another popular component is *vlad* or *volod* with connotations of "rule," "sway." There are four Vladimirs (Vl. I, "the Saint," d. 1015; Vl. II,

"Monomachus," d. 1125; Vl. of Putivl, Igor's son, d. 1212; and Vl., son of Mstislav of Smolensk) and six Vsevolods (Vs. I, d. 1092; Vs. II, d. 1146; Vs. of Suzdal, d. 1212; Vs., Igor's brother, d. 1196; Vs., a descendant of Vseslav of Polotsk; and Vs., a descendant of Mstislav I). Russian students learn to group princes by the pluralized patronymics of a celebrated ancestor (e.g., Yaroslavichi) into "nests" or "houses," and it will be seen that our bard is directly concerned with the House of Oleg (Ol'govichi), while his predecessor the bard Boyan seems to have been particularly interested in the House of Polotsk.

INDEX

The names and patronymics of Russian princes mentioned in The Song.

Boris Vyacheslavich, line 245.
Bryachislav Vasil'kovich, line 605.

David Rostislavich, lines 511, 685.

Efrosiniya Yaroslavna, see *Yaroslavna*.

Glyebov (Glyebovich), see *Volodimir*.
Glyeboví (Glyebovichi), line 510.
Glyebovna, line 229.

Igor' Svyatoslavich, lines 4-5, 42, 61, 71, 73, 91, 94, 111, 131, 170,
285, 290, 326, 351-352, 378, 383, 455, 521-522, 540-541,
560, 565, 581-582, 733, 738-740, 745-746, 752, 766, 772,
776, 804, 840, 842, 847, 854.
Ingvar Yaroslavich, line 571.
Izyaslav Vasil'kovich, line 591.
Izyaslav (I) Yaroslavich, see *Svyatopolk*.

Mstislav Rostislavich, line 572.
Mstislav Vladimirovich, line 26.
Mstislav Yaroslavich, line 542.

Oleg Igorevich, line 428.
Oleg Svyatoslavich, lines 172, 233-234, 235, 249, 255, 834.
Ol'ga Glyebovna, see *Glyebovna*.

Roman Mstislavich, line 542.
Roman Svyatoslavich, lines 29-30.
Rostislav Vsevolodich, lines 797, 800.
Ryurik (Rurik) *Rostislavich*, lines 511, 685.

Svyatopolk (II) Izyaslavich, line 252.
Svyatoslav Igorevich, line 428.
Svyatoslav (III) Vsevolodich, lines 356, 370, 376, 391, 451, 715.
Svyatoslav (II) Yaroslavich, line 834.

Vladimir Igorevich, line 856.
Vladimir (I) Svyatoslavich, lines 41, 682.
Vladimir (II) Vsevolodich, line 242.
Volodimir Glyebovich, lines 494, 496.
Vseslav Bryachislavich, lines 595, 617, 627, 632, 659.
Vsevolod Svyatoslavich, lines 71, 72, 211, 221, 286, 351-352, 455,
    855.
Vsevolod Vasil'kovich, line 606.
Vsevolod Yaroslavich, line 571.
Vsevolod Yurievich, line 497.

Yaroslav Svyatoslavich, line 834.
Yaroslav (I) Vladimirovich, lines 25, 232, 241, 648.
Yaroslav Volodimirkovich, lines 523, 617.
Yaroslav Vsevolodich, line 470.
Yaroslavna, lines 688, 697, 709, 720.

PEDIGREE OF
RUSSIAN TERRITORIAL PRINCES
in relation to
THE SONG OF IGOR'S CAMPAIGN

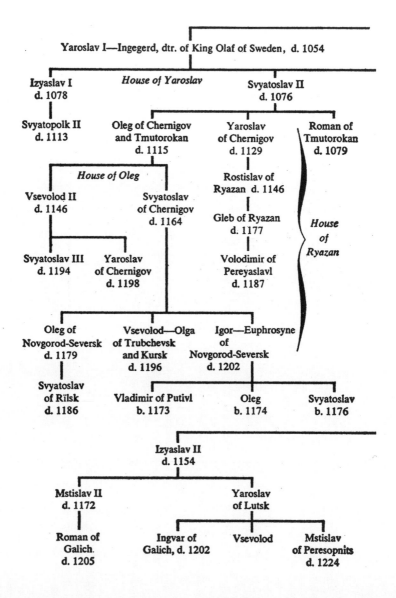

Yaroslav I—Ingegerd, dtr. of King Olaf of Sweden, d. 1054

House of Yaroslav

Izyaslav I
d. 1078

Svyatoslav II
d. 1076

Svyatopolk II
d. 1113

Oleg of Chernigov
and Tmutorokan
d. 1115

Yaroslav
of Chernigov
d. 1129

Roman of
Tmutorokan
d. 1079

House of Oleg

Rostislav of
Ryazan d. 1146

Vsevolod II
d. 1146

Svyatoslav
of Chernigov
d. 1164

Gleb of Ryazan
d. 1177

*House
of
Ryazan*

Svyatoslav III
d. 1194

Yaroslav
of Chernigov
d. 1198

Volodimir of
Pereyaslavl
d. 1187

Oleg of
Novgorod-Seversk
d. 1179

Vsevolod—Olga
of Trubchevsk
and Kursk
d. 1196

Igor—Euphrosyne
of
Novgorod-Seversk
d. 1202

Svyatoslav
of Rïlsk
d. 1186

Vladimir of Putivl
b. 1173

Oleg
b. 1174

Svyatoslav
b. 1176

Izyaslav II
d. 1154

Mstislav II
d. 1172

Yaroslav
of Lutsk

Roman of
Galich.
d. 1205

Ingvar of
Galich, d. 1202

Vsevolod

Mstislav
of Peresopnits
d. 1224

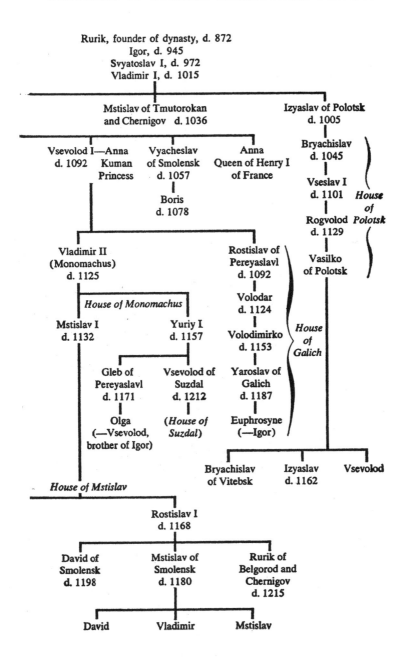

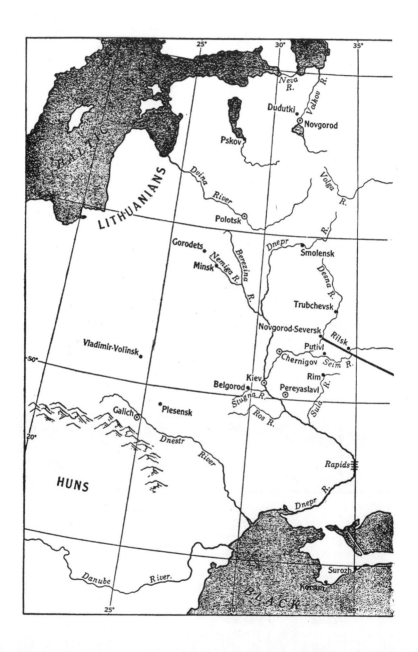

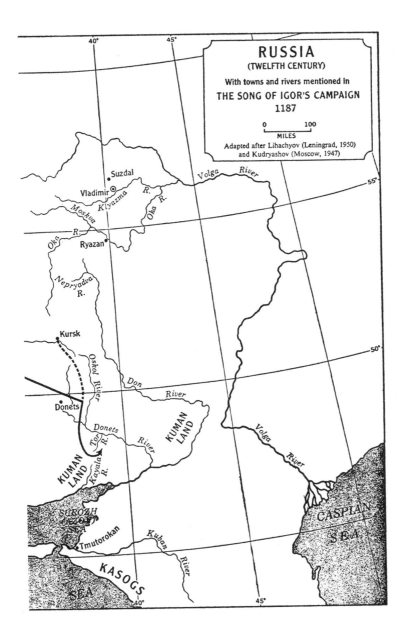

RUSSIA
(TWELFTH CENTURY)

With towns and rivers mentioned in

THE SONG OF IGOR'S CAMPAIGN
1187

0   100
MILES
Adapted after Lihachyov (Leningrad, 1950)
and Kudryashov (Moscow, 1947)

Suzdal

Vladimir

Klyazma R.

Moskva

Oka R.

Volga River

Oka R.

Ryazan

Nepryadva R.

Kursk

Oskol River

Don River

Donets

Donets River

KUMAN LAND

Tor R.

Kayala R.

KUMAN LAND

Volga River

SUROZH (AZOV) SEA

Tmutorokan

Kuban River

CASPIAN SEA

KASOGS

SEA

THE SONG OF
IGOR'S CAMPAIGN,
IGOR SON OF SVYATOSLAV
AND GRANDSON OF OLEG.

Exordium   Might it not become us, brothers,
to begin in the diction of yore
the stern tale
of the campaign of Igor,
5 Igor son of Svyatoslav?

Let us, however,
begin this song
in keeping with the happenings
of these times
10 and not with the contriving of Boyan.

Exordium
(continued)

For he, vatic Boyan,
if he wished to make a laud for one,
ranged in thought
[like the nightingale] over the tree;
15   like the gray wolf
across land;
like the smoky eagle
up to the clouds.

For as he recalled, said he,
20   the feuds of initial times,
"He set ten falcons
upon a flock of swans,
and the one first overtaken,
sang a song first"—
25   to Yaroslav of yore,
and to brave Mstislav
who slew Rededya
before the Kasog troops,
and to fair Roman
30   son of Svyatoslav.

Exordium
(concluded)

To be sure, brothers,
Boyan did not [really]
set ten falcons
upon a flock of swans:
35   his own vatic fingers
he laid on the live strings,
which then twanged out by themselves
a paean to princes.

So let us begin, brothers,
40   this tale—
from Vladimir of yore
to nowadays Igor,
who girded his mind
with fortitude,
45   and sharpened his heart
with manliness;
[thus] imbued with the spirit of arms,
he led his brave troops
against the Kuman land
50   in the name of the Russian land.

Boyan
apostrophized

O Boyan, nightingale
of the times of old!
If *you* were to trill [your praise of]
   these troops,
while hopping, nightingale,
55   over the tree of thought;
[if you were] flying in mind
up to the clouds;
[if] weaving paeans around *these* times,
[*you* were] roving the Troyan Trail,
60   across fields onto hills;
then the song to be sung of Igor,
that grandson of Oleg [, would be]:

"No storm has swept falcons across
   wide fields;
flocks of daws flee toward the Great
   Don";
65   or you might intone thus,
vatic Boyan, grandson of Veles:
"Steeds neigh beyond the Sula;
glory rings in Kiev;
trumpets blare in Novgorod [-Seversk];
70   banners are raised in Putivl."

Vsevolod's
speech

Igor waits for his dear brother
    Vsevolod.

And Wild Bull Vsevolod [arrives and]
    says to him:
"My one brother, one bright brightness,
    you Igor!
We both are Svyatoslav's sons.

75   Saddle, brother, your swift steeds.
As to mine, they are ready,
saddled ahead, near Kursk;
as to my Kurskers, they are famous
    knights—
swaddled under war-horns,

80   nursed under helmets,
fed from the point of the lance;
to them the trails are familiar,
to them the ravines are known,
the bows they have are strung tight,

85   the quivers, unclosed,
the sabers, sharpened;
themselves, like gray wolves,
they lope in the field,
seeking for themselves honor,

90   and for their prince glory."

The Eclipse
and Igor's
speech

Then Igor glanced up at the bright sun
and saw that from it with darkness
his warriors were covered.
And Igor says to his Guards:
95   "Brothers and Guards!
It is better indeed to be slain
than to be enslaved;
so let us mount, brothers,
upon our swift steeds,
100   and take a look at the blue Don."

A longing consumed the prince's mind,
and the omen was screened from him
by the urge to taste
of the Great Don:
105   "For I wish," he said,
"to break a lance
on the limit of the Kuman field;
with you, sons of Rus, I wish
either to lay down my head
110   or drink a helmetful of the Don."

Igor sets out;
accumulation
of omens

Then Igor set foot
in the golden stirrup
and rode out in the champaign.
The sun blocks his way with darkness.

115   Night, moaning ominously unto him,
awakens the birds;
the whistling of beasts [arises?];
[stirring?] the daeva calls
on the top of a tree,

120   bids hearken the land unknown—
the Volga,
and the [Azov] Seaboard,
and the Sula country,
and Surozh,

125   and Korsun,
and you, idol of Tmutorokan!

Meanwhile by untrodden roads
the Kumans make for the Great Don;
[their] wagons screak in the middle of
    night;

130   one might say—dispersed swans.

Igor rides on Igor leads Donward his warriors.
His misfortunes already
are forefelt by the birds in the
   oakscrub.
The wolves, in the ravines,
135 conjure the storm.
The erns with their squalling
summon the beasts to the bones.
The foxes yelp
at the vermilion shields.
140 O Russian land,
you are already behind the culmen!

Long does the night keep darkling.
Dawn sheds its light.
Mist has covered the fields.
145 Stilled is the trilling of nightingales;
the jargon of jackdaws has woken.
With their vermilion shields
the sons of Rus have barred the great
   prairie,
seeking for themselves honor,
150 and for their prince glory.

The first
engagement

Early on Friday
they trampled the pagan Kuman troops
and fanned out like arrows
over the field;
155 they bore off fair Kuman maidens
and, with them, gold,
and brocades,
and precious samites.
By means of caparisons,
160 and mantlets,
and furred cloaks of leather
they started making plankings
to plank marshes
and miry spots
165 with all kinds of Kuman weaves.

A vermilion standard,
a white gonfalon,
a vermilion penant of [dyed] horsehair
and a silver hilt
170 [went] to [Igor] son of Svyatoslav.

*Night, and
dawn of
Saturday*

In the field slumbers
Oleg's brave aerie:
far has it flown!
Not born was it to be wronged
175   either by falcon or hawk,
or by you, black raven,
pagan Kuman!
Gzak runs like a gray wolf;
Konchak lays out a track for him
180   to the Great Don.

On the next day very early
bloody effulgences
herald the light.
Black clouds come from the sea:
185   They want to cover
the four suns,
and in them throb blue lightnings.
There is to be great thunder,
there is to come rain in [the guise of]
    arrows
190   from the Great Don.

Saturday:
the Kumans
counterattack

Here lances shall break,
here sabers shall blunt
against Kuman helmets,
on the river Kayala by the Great Don.

195 O Russian land,
you are already behind the culmen!

Now the winds, Stribog's grandsons,
in [the guise of] arrows waft from the
sea
against the brave troops of Igor!

200 The earth rumbles,
the rivers run sludgily,
dust covers the fields.
The banners speak:
"The Kumans are coming

205 from the Don and from the sea and
from all sides!"
The Russian troops retreat.
The Fiend's children bar the field
with their war cries;
the brave sons of Rus bar it

210 with their vermilion shields.

Vsevolod   Fierce Bull Vsevolod!
in battle   You stand your ground,
           you spurt arrows at warriors,
           you clang on helmets
215   with swords of steel.
           Wherever the Bull bounds,
           darting light from his golden helmet,
           there lie pagan Kuman heads:
           cleft with tempered sabers
220   are [their] Avar helmets—
           by you, Fierce Bull Vsevolod!

           What wound, brothers,
           can matter to one
           who has forgotten
225   honors and life,
           and the town of Chernigov—
           golden throne of his fathers—
           and of his dear beloved,
           Gleb's fair daughter,
230   the wonts and ways!

Recollections of
Oleg's feuds

There have been the ages of Troyan;
gone are the years of Yaroslav;
there have been the campaigns of Oleg,
Oleg son of Svyatoslav.

235 *That* Oleg forged feuds with the sword,
and sowed the land with arrows.
He sets foot in the golden stirrup
in the town of Tmutorokan:
a similar clinking

240 had been hearkened
by the great Yaroslav of long ago;
and Vladimir son of Vsevolod
every morn [that he heard it]
stopped his ears in Chernigov.

245 As to Boris son of Vyacheslav,
vainglory brought him to judgment
and on the Kanin [river]
spread out a green pall,
for the offense against Oleg,

250 the brave young prince.

Recollections of
Oleg's feuds
(continued)

And from *that* Kayala
Svyatopolk had his father conveyed
—cradled between Hungarian pacers
  [tandemwise]—
to St. Sophia in Kiev.

255   Then, under Oleg, child of Malglory,
sown were and sprouted discords;
perished the livelihood
of Dazhbog's grandson
among princely feuds;
260   human ages dwindled.
Then, across the Russian land,
seldom did plowmen shout [hup-hup
  to their horses]
but often did ravens croak
as they divided among themselves the
  cadavers,
265   while jackdaws announced in their
  own jargon
that they were about to fly to the feed.
Thus it was in those combats
and in those campaigns,
but such a battle
270   had never been heard of.

*Termination
of battle* From early morn to eve,
and from eve to dawn,
tempered arrows fly,
sabers resound against helmets,
275 steel lances crack.
In the field unknown, midst the
Kuman land,
the black sod under hooves
was sown with bones
and irrigated with gore.
280 As grief they came up
throughout the Russian land.

What dins unto me,
what rings unto me?
Early today, before the effulgences,
285 Igor turns back his troops:
he is anxious about his dear brother
Vsevolod.
They fought one day;
they fought another;
on the third, toward noon,
290 Igor's banners fell.

Defeat and
Lamentations   Here the brothers parted
              on the bank of the swift Kayala.
              Here was a want of blood-wine;
              here the brave sons of Rus
295   finished the feast—
              got their in-laws drunk,
              and themselves lay down
              in defense of the Russian land.

              The grass droops with condolements
300   and the tree with sorrow
              bends to the ground.
              For now, brothers, a cheerless tide has
                  set in;
              now the wild has covered the strong;
              Wrong has risen among the forces
305   of Dazhbog's grandson;
              in the guise of a maiden
              [Wrong] has stepped into Troyan's
                  land;
              she clapped her swan wings
              on the blue sea by the Don,
310   [and] clapping, decreased rich times.

Lamentations
(continued)

The strife of the princes
against the pagans
has come to an end,
for brother says to brother:

315 "This is mine,
and that is mine too,"
and the princes have begun to say
of what is small:
"This is big,"

320 while against their own selves
they forge discord,
[and] while from all sides with victories
the pagans enter the Russian land.

O, far has the falcon gone, slaying
birds:

325 to the sea!
But Igor's brave troops
cannot be brought back to life.
In their wake the Keener has wailed,
and Lamentation has overrun the
Russian land,

330 shaking the embers in the inglehorn.

Lamentations
(concluded)

The Russian women
have started to weep, repeating:
"Henceforth our dear husbands
cannot be thought of by [our] thinking,
335   nor mused about by [our] musing,
nor beheld with [our] eyes;
as to gold and silver
none at all shall we touch!"

And, brothers, Kiev groaned in sorrow,
340   and so did Chernigov in adversity;
anguish spread flowing
over the Russian land;
abundant woe made its way
midst the Russian land,
345   while the princes forged discord
against their own selves,
[and] while the pagans, with victories
prowling over the Russian land,
took tribute of one vair
350   from every homestead.

Victories of
Svyatoslav III
recalled

All because the two brave sons of
    Svyatoslav,
Igor and Vsevolod,
stirred up the virulence
that had been all but curbed
355   by their senior,
dread Svyatoslav, the Great [Prince] of
    Kiev,
[who kept the Kumans] in dread.

He beat down [the Kumans] with his
    mighty troops
and steel swords;
360   invaded the Kuman land;
leveled underfoot
hills and ravines;
muddied rivers and lakes;
drained torrents and marshes;
365   and the pagan Kobyaka,
out of the Bight of the Sea,
from among the great iron Kuman
    troops,
he plucked like a tornado,
and Kobyaka dropped in the town of
    Kiev,
370   in the guard-room of Svyatoslav!

Igor blamed   Now the Germans,
and the Venetians,
now the Greeks,
and the Moravians
375 sing glory
to Svyatoslav,
but chide
Prince Igor,
for he let abundance sink
380 to the bottom of the Kayala,
[and] filled up Kuman rivers
with Russian gold.

Now Igor the prince
has switched
385 from a saddle of gold
to a thrall's saddle.
Pined away
have the ramparts of towns,
and merriment
390 has drooped.

Svyatoslav's
dream

And Svyatoslav saw a troubled dream
in Kiev upon the hills:
"This night, from eventide,
they dressed me," he said, "with a black
  pall
395 on a bedstead of yew.
They ladled out for me
blue wine mixed with bane.
From the empty quivers
of pagan tulks
400 they rolled great pearls
onto my breast,
and caressed me.
Already the traves
lacked the master-girder
405 in my gold-crested tower!

All night, from eventide,
demon ravens croaked.
On the outskirts of Plesensk
there was a logging sleigh,
410 and it was carried to the blue sea!"

The Boyars
explain their
sovereign's
dream

And the boyars said to the Prince:
"Already, Prince, grief has enthralled
     the mind;
for indeed two falcons
have flown off the golden paternal, throne
     throne
415 in quest of the town of Tmutorokan—
or at least to drink a helmetful of the
     Don.
Already the falcons' winglets
have been clipped
by the pagans' sabers,
420 and the birds themselves
entangled in iron meshes."

Indeed, dark it was
on the third day [of battle]:
two suns were murked,
425 both crimson pillars
were extinguished,
and with them both young moons,
Oleg and Svyatoslav,
were veiled with darkness
430 and sank in the sea.

The Boyar's
speech
(continued)

"On the river Kayala
darkness has covered the light.
Over the Russian land
the Kumans have spread,

435 like a brood of pards,
and great turbulence
imparted to the Hin.

"Already disgrace
has come down upon glory.

440 Already thralldom
has crashed down upon freedom.
Already the daeva
has swooped down upon the land.
And lo! Gothic fair maids

445 have burst into song
on the shore of the blue sea:
chinking Russian gold,
they sing demon times;
they lilt vengeance for Sharokan;

450 and already we, [your] Guards, hanker
after mirth."

Svyatoslav's
speech

Then the great Svyatoslav
let fall a golden word
mingled with tears,
and he said:

455   "O my juniors, Igor and Vsevolod!
Early did you begin
to worry with swords the Kuman land,
and seek personal glory;
but not honorably you triumphed

460   for not honorably you shed
pagan blood.
Your brave hearts are forged of hard
    steel
and proven in turbulence;
[but] what is this you have done

465   to my silver hoarness!

"Nor do I see any longer
the sway of my strong,
and wealthy,
and multimilitant

470   brother Yaroslav—

Svyatoslav's speech (continued)

with his Chernigov boyars,
with his Moguts, and Tatrans,
and Shelbirs, and Topchaks,
and Revugs, and Olbers;
475 for they without bucklers,
with knives in the legs of their boots,
vanquish armies with war cries,
to the ringing of ancestral glory.

"But you said:
480 'Let us be heroes on our own,
let us by ourselves grasp the anterior
glory
and by ourselves share the posterior
one.'
Now is it so wonderful, brothers,
for an old man to grow young?
485 When a falcon has moulted,
he drives birds on high:
he does not allow any harm
to befall his nest;
but here is the trouble:
490 princes are of no help to me."

The Author
apostrophizes
contempora-
neous princes

Inside out have the times turned.
Now in Rim [people] scream
under Kuman sabers,
and Volodimir [screams]
495 under wounding blows.
Woe and anguish to you, [Volodimir]
son of Gleb!

Great prince Vsevolod!
Do you not think of flying here from
afar
to safeguard the paternal golden
throne?
500 For you can with your oars
scatter in drops the Volga,
and with your helmets
scoop dry the Don.
If you were here,
505 a female slave would fetch
one nogata,
and a male slave,
one rezana;
for you can shoot on land live bolts—
510 [these are] the bold sons of Gleb!

Apostrophe
(continued)

You turbulent Rurik, and [you] David!
Were not your men's gilt helmets
afloat on blood?
Do not your brave knights roar like
  bulls
515 wounded by tempered sabers
in the field unknown?
Set your feet, my lords,
in your stirrups of gold
to avenge the wrong of our time,
520 the Russian land,
and the wounds of Igor,
turbulent son of Svyatoslav.

Eight-minded Yaroslav of Galich!
You sit high on your gold-forged
  throne;
525 you have braced the Hungarian
  mountains
with your iron troops;
you have barred the [Hungarian] king's
  path;
you have closed the Danube's gates,
hurling weighty missiles over the clouds,
530 spreading your courts to the Danube.

Apostrophe
(continued)

Your thunders range
over lands;
you open Kiev's gates;
from the paternal golden throne
535   you shoot at sultans
beyond the lands.
Shoot [your arrows], lord,
at Konchak, the pagan slave,
to avenge the Russian land,
540   and the wounds of Igor,
turbulent son of Svyatoslav!

And you, turbulent Roman, and
  Mstislav!
A brave thought
carries your minds to deeds.
545   On high you soar to deeds
in your turbulence,
like the falcon
that rides the winds
as he strives in turbulence
550   to overcome the bird.

Apostrophe
(continued)   For you have iron breastplates
           under Latin helmets;
           these have made the earth rumble,
           and many nations—

555   Hins, Lithuanians, Yatvangians,
           Dermners, and Kumans—
           have dropped their spears
           and bowed their heads
           beneath those steel swords.

560   But already, [O] Prince Igor,
           the sunlight has dimmed,
           and, not goodly, the tree sheds its
               foliage.
           Along the Ros and the Sula
           the towns have been distributed;

565   and Igor's brave troops
           cannot be brought back to life!
           The Don, Prince, calls you,
           and summons the princes to victory.
           The brave princes, descendants of
               Oleg,

570   have hastened to fight.

Apostrophe
(continued)

Ingvar and Vsevolod,
and all three sons of Mstislav,
six-winged [hawks?] of no mean brood!
Not by victorious sorts

575 did you grasp your patrimonies.
Where, then, are your golden helmets,
and Polish spears, and shields?
Bar the gates of the prairie
with your sharp arrows

580 to avenge the Russian land
and the wounds of Igor,
turbulent son of Svyatoslav.

No longer indeed does the Sula flow
in silvery streams

585 for [the defense of] the town of
Pereyaslavl;
and the Dvina, too,
flows marsh-like
for the erstwhile dreaded
townsmen of Polotsk

590 to the war cries of pagans.

Izyaslav
recalled

Alone Izyaslav son of Vasilko
made his sharp swords ring
against Lithuanian helmets—
[only] to cut down the glory
595 of his grandsire Vseslav,
and himself he was cut down
by Lithuanian swords
under [his] vermilion shields,
[and fell] on the gory grass
600 [as if?] with a beloved one upon a bed

And [Boyan] said:
"Your Guards, Prince,
birds have hooded with their wings
and beasts have licked up their blood."
605 Neither your brother Bryachislav
nor your other one—Vsevolod—was
     there;
thus all alone
you let your pearly soul drop
out of your brave body
610 through your golden gorget.

Conclusion of
Apostrophe

Despondent
are the voices;
drooped
has merriment;
615 [only?] blare
the town trumpets.

Yaroslav, and all the descendants of
Vseslav!
The time has come
to lower your banners,
620 to sheathe your dented swords.
For you have already departed
from the ancestral glory;
for with your feuds
you started to draw the pagans
625 onto the Russian land,
onto the livelihood
of Vseslav.
Indeed, because of those quarrels
violence came
630 from the Kuman land.

Vseslav's fate In the seventh age of Troyan,
recalled   Vseslav cast lots
                 for the damsel he wooed.
                 By subterfuge,
635   propping himself upon mounted
                     troops,
                 he vaulted toward the town of Kiev
                 and touched with the staff [of his lance]
                 the Kievan golden throne.

                 Like a fierce beast
640   he leapt away from them [the troops?],
                 at midnight,
                 out of Belgorod,
                 having enveloped himself
                 in a blue mist.
645   Then at morn,
                 he drove in his battle axes,
                 opened the gates of Novgorod,
                 shattered the glory of Yaroslav,
                 [and] loped like a wolf
650   to the Nemiga from Dudutki.

Vseslav's fate
(continued)

On the Nemiga the spread sheaves
are heads,
the flails that thresh
are of steel,

655 lives are laid out on the threshing floor,
souls are winnowed from bodies.
Nemiga's gory banks are not sowed
goodly—
sown with the bones of Russia's sons.

Vseslav the prince judged men;
660 as prince, he ruled towns;
but at night he prowled
in the guise of a wolf.
From Kiev, prowling, he reached,
before the cocks [crew], Tmutorokan.
665 The path of Great Hors,
as a wolf, prowling, he crossed.
For him in Polotsk
they rang for matins early
at St. Sophia the bells;
670 but he heard the ringing in Kiev.

Vseslav's fate
(concluded)   Although, indeed, he had
a vatic soul in a doughty body,
he often suffered calamities.
Of him vatic Boyan
675   once said, with sense, in the tag:
"Neither the guileful nor the skillful,
neither bird [nor bard],
can escape God's judgment."
Alas! The Russian land shall moan
680   recalling her first years
and first princes!
Vladimir of yore, he,
could not be nailed to the Kievan hills.
Now some of his banners
685   have gone to Rurik and others to David,
but their plumes wave in counterturn.

Lances hum on the Dunay.
The voice of Yaroslav's daughter is
    heard;
like a cuckoo, [unto the field?]
    unknown,
690   early she calls.

Euphrosyne's
incantation

"I will fly, like a cuckoo," she says,
"down the Dunay.
I will dip my beaver sleeve
in the river Kayala.

695   I will wipe the bleeding wounds
on the prince's hardy body."
Yaroslav's daughter early weeps,
in Putivl on the rampart, repeating:

"Wind, Great Wind!

700   Why, lord, blow perversely?
Why carry those Hinish dartlets
on your light winglets
against my husband's warriors?
Are you not satisfied

705   to blow on high, up to the clouds,
rocking the ships upon the blue sea?
Why, lord, have you dispersed
my gladness all over the feather grass?"
Yaroslav's daughter early weeps,

710   in Putivl on the rampart, repeating:

Incantation
(continued)   "O Dnepr, famed one!
                  You have pierced stone hills
                  through the Kuman land.
                  You have lolled upon you
715   Svyatoslav's galleys
                  as far as Kobyaka's camp.
                  Loll up to me, lord, my husband
                  that I may not send my tears
                  seaward thus early."
720   Yaroslav's daughter early weeps,
                  in Putivl on the rampart, repeating:

                  "Bright and thrice-bright Sun!
                  To all you are warm and comely;
                  Why spread, lord, your scorching rays
725   on [my] husband's warriors;
                  [why] in the waterless field
                  parch their bows
                  with thirst,
                  close their quivers
730   with anguish?"

Igor's escape   The sea plashed at midnight;
                    waterspouts advance in mists;
                    God [?] points out to Igor
                    the way from the Kuman land
735   to the Russian land,
                    to the paternal golden throne.

                    The evening glow has faded:
                    Igor sleeps;
                    Igor keeps vigil;
740   Igor in thought measures the plains
                    from the Great Don
                    to the Little Donets;
                    [bringing] a horse at midnight,
                    Ovlur whistled beyond the river:
745   he bids Igor heed—
                    Igor is not to be [held in bondage].
                    [Ovlur] called,
                    the earth rumbled,
                    the grass swished,
750   the Kuman tents stirred.

Igor's escape   Meanwhile, like an ermine,
(continued)   Igor has sped to the reeds,
                    and [settled] upon the water
                    like a white duck.
755   He leaped upon the swift steed,
                    and sprang off it,
                    [and ran on,] like a demon wolf,
                    and sped to the meadowland of the
                        Donets,
                    and, like a falcon,
760   flew up to the mists,
                    killing geese
                    and swans,
                    for lunch,
                    and for dinner,
765   and for supper.

                    And even as Igor, like a falcon, flew,
                    Vlur, like a wolf, sped,
                    shaking off by his passage the cold
                        dew;
                    for both had worn out
770   their swift steeds.

Igor's escape　　Says the Donets:
(continued)　　"Prince Igor!
　　　　　　　Not small is your magnification,
　　　　　　　and Konchak's detestation,
775　　　　and the Russian land's gladness."

　　　　　　　Igor says:
　　　　　　　"O Donets!
　　　　　　　Not small is *your* magnification:
　　　　　　　you it was who lolled
780　　　　a prince on [your] waves;
　　　　　　　who carpeted for him
　　　　　　　with green grass
　　　　　　　your silver banks;
　　　　　　　who clothed him
785　　　　with warm mists
　　　　　　　under the shelter of the green tree;
　　　　　　　who had him guarded
　　　　　　　by the golden-eye on the water,
　　　　　　　the gulls on the currents,
790　　　　the [crested] black ducks on the winds.

Igor's escape
(continued)

Not like that," says [Igor],
"is the river Stugna:
endowed with a meager stream,
having fed [therefore]

795 on alien tills and runnels,
she rent between bushes
a youth, prince Rostislav,
imprisoning him.
On the Dnepr's dark bank

800 Rostislav's mother weeps the youth.
Pined away have the flowers with
    condolement,
and the tree has been bent to the
    ground with sorrow."

No chattering magpies are these:
on Igor's trail

805 Gzak and Konchak come riding.
Then the ravens did not caw,
the grackles were still,
the [real] magpies did not chatter;
only the woodpeckers, in the osiers
    climbing,

810 with taps marked [for Igor] the way to
    the river.

*Igor's escape
(continued)*

The nightingales
with gay songs
announce the dawn.

Says Gzak to Konchak:
815 "Since the falcon to his nest is flying,
let us shoot dead the falcon's son
with our gilded arrows."
Says Konchak to Gza [*sic*]:
"Since the falcon to his nest is flying,
820 why, let us entoil the falconet
by means of a fair maiden."
And says Gzak to Konchak:
"If we entoil him
by means of a fair maiden,
825 neither the falconet,
nor the fair maiden,
shall we have,
while the birds will start
to beat us
830 in the Kuman field."

Igor's return   Said Boyan, song-maker
of the times of old,
[of the campaigns] of the kogans
—Svyatoslav, Yaroslav, Oleg:
835   "Hard as it is for the head
to be without shoulders
bad it is for the body
to be without head,"
—for the Russian land
840   to be without Igor.

The sun shines in the sky:
Prince Igor is on Russian soil.
Maidens sing on the Danube;
[their?] voices weave
845   across the sea
to Kiev.
Igor rides up the Borichev [slope]
to the Blessed Virgin of the Tower;
countries rejoice,
850   cities are merry.

Conclusion After singing a song
     to the old princes
     one must then sing to the young:

     Glory to Igor son of Svyatoslav;
855   to Wild Bull Vsevolod;
     to Vladimir son of Igor!
     Hail, princes and knights
     fighting for the Christians
     against the pagan troops!
860   To the princes glory, and to the knights
      [glory]—Amen.

NOTES TO FOREWORD

1. The Ipatiev Chronicle *(Ipat'evskaya*—from the monastery of that name, where the chronicle, *letopis'*, was preserved) is a record covering four centuries from the beginnings of Russia to the end of the thirteenth century. It has 612 pages and is written, on paper, in a script pertaining to the fourteenth century. The first part contains the Kievan annals recording events of the twelfth century. This *Ipat'evskaya letopis'*, with the account of Igor's campaign under the year 6693 (A.D. 1185), has been published by the Archaeographic Commission in the *Polnoe sobranie Russkih lyetopisey* (Complete Collection of Russian Chronicles), St. P., 1843 (Second edition, 1908; Third edition, 1923). Another chronicle, the Lavrentiev one (*Letopis' po Lavrentievskomu Spisku*), which contains a much briefer account of Igor's campaign, under the wrong date 6694 (with correct days of the week), can be found in another publication of the same *Arheograficheskaya Kommissiya*, St. P., 1897.

2. The protagonist of The Song is the shadow of an actual contemporary of our bard who, for the rest, has greatly magnified the campaign of 1185. This glorified personage is Igor (1151-1202), at the time (since the death of his elder brother Oleg in 1179) prince of Novgorod-Seversk (a small town east of

Chernigov), grandson of Oleg prince of Chernigov and Tmutorokan, and son of Svyatoslav of Chernigov (d. 1164). In 1198, on the death of his first cousin Yaroslav of Chernigov, Igor became prince of that city. His first wife had born him five sons; his second wife was Euphrosyne, the Yaroslavna of The Song, daughter of Yaroslav of Galich. History remembers Igor as an insignificant, shifty and pugnacious prince.

3. Vsevolod, prince of Trubchevsk and Kursk—towns to the north and east of his brother Igor's seat (see Map). He died in 1196 and is remembered by the chronicler as the most valorous and the kindliest of the descendants of Oleg Malglory. His wife (the Glebovna of our Song) was presumably Olga daughter of Gleb of Pereyaslavl.

4. Svyatoslav of Rïlsk (1166-1186), son of Oleg prince of Novgorod-Seversk, Igor's brother.

5. Vladimir, prince of Putivl (1173-1212), eldest son of Igor.

6. During the period immediately following the death of Yaroslav I, in the second half of the eleventh century, three powerful princes reigned in Kievan Russia: Izyaslav I, son of Yaroslav, and his two brothers, Svyatoslav, at the time prince of Chernigov (later Svyatoslav II), and Vsevolod, at the time prince of Pereyaslavl (later Vsevolod I). It is at this time that the Kumans (whom Russian sources term *Polovtsï* or *Kïpchaki*) first invade the steppes between the Dnepr and the Volga. In their numerous forays of which at least fifty considerable ones can be counted between 1061 and 1210, they kept devastating Russian settlements in the southern parts of the Kievan region. It is also then, in the eleventh century, that begin the internecine feuds between the descendants of Yaroslav I. The worst offender was the founder of the house of Chernigov, Oleg Malglory (son of Svyatoslav II), Igor's grandfather, who waged bitter battles against his uncles and cousins (especially Vladimir Monomachus). Up to around 1180 Igor, like other descendants of Oleg Malglory, had pursued the

policy of concluding military alliances with the Kumans in order to conduct feuds with the descendants of Rostislav I. The Kumans disappear from the pages of history in the third decade of the thirteenth century when they are engulfed in the invasion of the Mongols (Tatars).

7. Svyatoslav III (d. 1194), son of Vsevolod II and grandson of Oleg Malglory, thus Igor's first cousin. His dominion was limited to the city of Kiev, the rest of the Kievan region being ruled by Rurik, son of Rostislav I, with whom he had routed the Kumans in 1183, without Igor's participation. Our bard exaggerates Svyatoslav's greatness and might.

8. Igor (who was wounded in the arm) and the three other princes were captured by four different Kuman chieftains, whose names are hopelessly Russianized by the chronicler: Chilbuk took Igor; Roman son of Kza took Vsevolod; Kopti took Vladimir; and Eldechyuk took Svyatoslav.

9. The accents are there merely to indicate the correct stress to the non-Russian reader. They are not shown in Russian. The Russian *"u"* is always pronounced as in "June," the *"i"* as in "Pisa" and the *"e"* (or the *"ye"*) as in "yes." The transliteration *"Igoreve"* is based on the modern (post-Revolution) Russian spelling. In old Russian another letter, arbitrarily represented by *"ye,"* and pronounced identically with *"e,"* replaced the latter in certain roots and endings. For the sake of exactitude I have kept this *"ye"* when transcribing the texts and titles in which it was used.

The original title of the work under consideration is: *Slovo o polku Igorevye, Igorya sïna Svyatoslavlya, vnuka Ol'gova* (as given in the First Edition, Moscow, 1800, p. 1). The obvious translation of *slovo* is "word," in the sense of "discourse," "oration," "sermon"; but these terms stress too heavily the didactic character of a work to the exclusion of its poetry. The term *"slovo"* is looser and more comprehensive than "discourse," etc., but it should be noted that the author himself, within his work, refers to it by means of other terms, such as "tale" (lines 3 and 40) and "song" (line 7). It is indeed a merging of prose and poetry, with apostrophic intonations of oratory mingling with the lyrical strain of melodious lamentations. Its peculiar lilt, with beats matching the breath of cadenced eloquence, is closer to rhythmic prose than to poetry. On the whole, and despite the lack of measure and rhyme, it must be classified, as its first editors did, as a *"chanson,"* a gest, a heroic song. It is too dramatic and elaborate to be termed a "lay," and the word "tale" is inadequate to cover the rich variety of its subject, where accounts of battles are interrupted by poetical and political digressions, and where the story is variegated with dialogues, and dreams, and incantations, and many other tricks of style. After a good deal of hesitation I have decided to call it "song," and have been moved in doing so by the final consideration that our author was above all a poet, and that, as in all literary masterpieces, only inspiration and art really matter.

10. This information is supplied by a casual footnote on page VII (penultimate) of Musin's introduction (entitled "The historical contents of the Song") to the First Edition (and is later amplified by Karamzin in his *History of Russia*, 1816, vol. 2, note 333, and vol. 3, notes 272 and 282). Eight titles are listed but they boil down to six works in all: two historical tracts containing the annals of ancient Russia; The Tale of Opulent India; The Tale of Akir the Wise; The Song of the Campaign of Igor; and the Acts and Life of Digenis Akritas (three titles), in this order.

11. According to a dignified but ridiculously inadequate letter, dated December 31, 1813, which Musin wrote to Kalaydovich in answer to a series of questions set by that scholar.

12. The date of the actual composition of The Song can be established more precisely than that of most European epics of the twelfth century. In a central passage our bard apostrophizes a number of contemporaneous princes among whom we find Volodimir of Pereyaslavl and Yaroslav of Galich. The first is

mentioned as severely wounded (494-496), and we know from the chronicle that he died of his wounds on April 18, 1187; the second is mentioned as flourishing (523-538), and we know that he died on October 1, 1187. We also know that Igor's escape from the Kuman camp took place in the spring or early summer of 1186, and that first he visited his principality (Novgorod-Seversk) and that of his uncle (Chernigov) before riding into Kiev (847-848). The end of The Song implies that the author is aware that Igor's son Vladimir of Putivl married, while in captivity, a Kuman princess; according to the chronicle he arrived home around St. Euphrosyne's day, September 25, 1187, with wife and child (this places his marriage in Kuman land not later than the middle of 1186).

It is pretty useless to deduce the life history and human form of a poet from his work; and the greater the artist the more likely it is for us to arrive at erroneous conclusions. It seems reasonable to suppose that our bard was a *druzhinnik*, a Kievan knight; but for all we know he might have been a learned monk taking a pagan vacation. We may suppose he was a courtier of Svyatoslav III of Kiev but it is just as likely that his home was Pereyaslavl in the Sula region or that he hailed from Kursk. He was evidently a keen sportsman with a fine knowledge of prairie fauna and flora and generally of the country from the Seim to the Azov Sea. It is possible that he took part in Igor's campaign, or in some phase of it.

13. Today, after a century and a half of comment and amendation, The Song has almost regained its (presumable) pristine clarity which generations of transcribers (including Musin's amanuensis) had impaired. Apart from several separate terms, the exact meaning of which is doubtful because probably misspelt by transcribers, there are only a few passages (such as lines 115-119, 406-410, 426-430, 599-601, 635-636, 794-799, 831-834) which are really hopelessly corrupted. A small number of words, usually

nonce words, remain obscure, and there is a remote chance that texts in other manuscripts may still come to light that will satisfactorily explain them.

14. After our lines 38, 150, 180, 687, 730, and 830. The apograph is more or less similarly punctuated by Musin's scribe, but is not paragraphed.

15. The Song occupies the left side of forty-six pages with the modern Russian version *en regard*. There are sixty-two footnotes, a list of four misprints, and a Pedigree of Princes. The editors lean heavily on the standard Russian history of the day, Vasiliy Tatishchev's *Istoriya Rossiyskaya s samih drevneyshih vremyon*—especially volume 3, published, after the author's death, by Miller in 1774. Facsimiles of this First Edition can be found in Adrianov-Peretts, 1950, and in Dmitriev, 1952.

16. As proven by Eleonski (in *Slovo o polku Igoreve*, Moscow, 1947, p. 96) the first allusion to *"Igoreva Pesn'"* (and to Boyan) occurs in Canto Sixteen of the third edition of Mihail Heraskov's epic "Vladimir [I]" as completed by him in November, 1796 and as published in his *Works*, Part 2, Moscow, January, 1797. This wretched poem is in Alexandrine couplets (following the French style). An asterisk prefixed to the lines

O bard of ancient years, boreal *Ossiyán*,

Self-buried in the ruins of centuries, *Bayán* [*sic*]

leads to the following footnote (*op. cit.* p. 301): "Recently there has been discovered a manuscript entitled *Pyesn'* (song) *o polku Igorevu* composed by an unknown writer, it seems, many centuries before our times [;] therein is mentioned Bayan [*sic*], the Russian songster."

In the same year, 1797, the October issue of *Le Spectateur du Nord*, a French émigré monthly journal published in Hamburg, Germany, carried a note written by its Russian correspondent, the historian Karamzin (in *Lettre au Spectateur sur la littérature russe*, signed N.N.) announcing the event thus: *"On a déterré, il y a deux ans, dans nos archives, le fragment d'un poème, intitulé le Chant des guerriers d'Igor* [a mistranslation of *polk*, taken here in the sense of "host" instead of the true "campaign"]." This would place the discovery in 1795. Following Heraskov's lead, Karamzin in his article compares "the ancient Russian bard" to Ossian and describes The Song in the following ludicrous manner: *"Le poète, traçant le tableau d'un combat sanglant, s'écrie: Ah! Je sens que mon pinceau est foible et languissant; je n'ai pas le talent du grand Bayan [sic], ce rossignol des temps passés."* The automatic terms used by Karamzin in describing The Song (*"fragment," "style énergique," "héroïsme sublime," "horreurs de la nature"*) are the stock-in-trade of French writers when speaking of Letourneur's *Ossian.*

Beyond the allusions to him by our bard (and by Sofoniy), nothing is known of this Boyan, a prophetically inclined Kievan minstrel who—judging by the dates pertaining to the princes he sang—must have flourished from 1035 to 1105, a tremendous span for a poet. Our bard deliberately quotes his great predecessor in lines 163 and 210, and perhaps in two other passages (4, 146). Moreover, he cunningly mimics Boyan's manner in order to introduce his own story (51-70).

Boyan is a name of southern Slav origin. A Bulgarian king (Simeon, d. 927) had a son Bayan (Baianus) who had been taught magic. By an amusing coincidence, in 1783, long before Boyan or Bayan had come to light, Vasiliy Lyovshin, author of the famous Russian Tales, while in the process of fabricating pretty feminine names hit upon "Bayana" (derived from *obayanie*, fascination, charm) for one of his princesses.

17. André Mazon, of the Collège de France, has attempted to turn the tables on time and prove that it is The Song that is an imitation of the *Zadonshchina.* His study (*Le Slovo d'Igor,* Paris, 1940, pp. 5-179), while containing many interesting juxtapositions, is fatally vitiated by his total incapacity of artistic appreciation. There is no great sin in calling The Song *"une oeuvre*

récente en forme de pastiche" (p. 41) but it is meaningless to contrast it as a work *"factice, incohérente et médiocre"* (p. 173) to the *Zadon-shchina* which Mazon describes as *"toujours sincère"* (a phrase used praisefully by people who do not understand art).

The *Zadonshchina* can be found in *Voinskie Povesti Drevney Rusi* (Military Tales of Ancient Rus), a collection edited by Miss Adrianov-Peretts, Leningrad, 1949.

18. I made a first attempt to translate *Slovo o Polku Igoreve* in 1952. My object was purely utilitarian—to provide my students with an English text. In that first version I followed uncritically Roman Jakobson's recension as published in *La Geste du Prince Igor*. Later, however, I grew dissatisfied not only with my own—much too "readable"—translation but also with Jakobson's views. Mimeographed copies of that obsolete version which are still in circulation at Cornell and Harvard should now be destroyed.

COMMENTARY

line

2   In the diction of yore: in an ancient style of speech, in outdated wording, *starïmi slovesï. Starïy* would mean today merely "old," but is used by our bard in a sense best rendered as "of old" or "of yore" (thus, for instance, in reference to former princes at 25 and 682).

3   Stern: *trudnïh.* In old Russian the word *trud* connotes not only "work" but also "grief," "pain," "endeavor" and the hardships of war.

4   Igor: see note 2 to Foreword.

8   In keeping with the happenings: *po bïlinam:* according to actual events, to facts and not to fiction.

10   In the *Zadonshchina,* Boyan is praised as *gorazdïy gudets v Kievye,* the skillful Kievan bard. While singing or reciting, the *gudets* played *(gudel)* on the *gusli,* a kind of small horizontal harp or cithara, of ten strings (judging by a vignette of 1358 reproduced in

83

line

La Geste du Prince Igor, p. 181). Except for The Song (and the obviously imitative *Zadonshchina*) there is no known work mentioning Boyan. He must have died around 1105 (see also note 16 to Foreword).

11 Vatic (from Latin *vates*, a seer, a prophet): *veshchiy;* thus endowed with the power not only of inspiration but of magic.

13-14 In thought over the tree: *mïsliyu po drevu.* This has taxed the scholarship and artfulness of numerous commentators. At least two species of squirrel (evolved from *mïs'*, mouse) have been made to perform in the branches of the metaphor. But apart from the fact that the same image in another form occurs at 55, and that a genuine squirrel is properly named *belya* at 349, it seems clear that the logical or clerical lacuna here between "thought" and "tree" should be filled with *slaviem* ("in the guise of a nightingale"), thus completing the triple formula (the first member of which is explicitly supplied by 54). Some commentators have treated, here and elsewhere, the tree, *drevo*, synecdochically (in the sense of "timber," "grove," "wood"), but this only blurs the clear-cut quality of the image in relation to "branching thought."

17 Smoky: this seems the simplest way of translating *shizïy* (now *sizïy*), smoke-colored, dove-gray, blue-gray, slate-blue, the dimness of dusk, the tint of distance.

line

21-24   The image of the ten falcons pursuing swans is the first of a series of metaphors borrowed from the hunt. The St. Cyril text of the *Zadonshchina* has the silly "his golden fingers on the live strings," while the Synod text turns this into the still sillier "his white hands on the golden strings."

25-30   The three princes named here are: Igor's great-great-grandfather, Yaroslav I, the Wise (d. 1054), son of Vladimir I; Yaroslav's brother, Mstislav of Tmutorokan (d. 1036); and Yaroslav's grandson, Roman of Tmutorokan (d. 1079); son of Svyatoslav II and brother of Igor's grandfather, Oleg Malglory. During a campaign which Mstislav undertook in 1022 against the Kasogs (a Caucasian tribe related to the Circassians), their leader Rededia, when both hosts confronted each other, challenged him to a wrestling match—instead of having their troops wage a bloody battle. In the course of the contest, Mstislav discovered that Rededia was stronger than he and, after a quick prayer to the Virgin, produced a knife, and dispatched the poor giant.

41   Presumably Vladimir I, the Saint (d. 1015) who baptized Russia in 988.

48   The historical Igor set out for the Donets rivershed from his princedom of Novgorod-Seversk on April 23, 1185. He intended to reach the Don (some 500 miles to the southeast), and even Tmutorokan (another 200 miles south) but actually did not get

line

further than the prairie south of the Donets (some 400 miles southeast of Novgorod-Seversk).

49   See note 6 to Foreword.

50   In the name: for the defense of, for the sake of, on behalf of, for the Russian land, *za zemlyu rus'kuyu*. The phrase also occurs at 298; but at 539 and 580 the same particle assumes a meaning of "to avenge." Other references to the "Russian land" occur in 140, 195, 261, 281, 298, 323, 329, 342, 433, 625, 679, 735, 775, 839 and 842. In the last passage, *v Ruskoy zemli*, the translation "on Russian soil" seems the closest (*zemlya* meaning both land and earth, extent and essence).

51-70   I follow Sobolevski and other scholars (see Gudziy in the collection *Slovo o polku Igoreve* edited by Adrianov-Peretts, 1950) in assuming that a page was transposed by mistake in the lost manuscript book from which the First Edition and the Archival Apograph took their text. I do this from considerations of artistic structure, not of historical sequence as given in the Ipatiev Chronicle (to which no manipulation neither can nor need make The Song conform). In the First Edition and in the Apograph the line corresponding to my line 50, and concluding, as I think, page 3 of the lost manuscript, is followed by the passage corresponding to my lines 91-110 (solar eclipse and Igor's speech), after which come the lines corresponding to my 51-70 (apostrophe

line

to Boyan), then 71-90 (the wait for Vsevolod and his speech), and 111-130 (Igor's departure and the omens). Surely, the apostrophe to Boyan (51-70) must come immediately after the evocation of his style and the settling of the theme of The Song (31-50); and, on the other hand, Igor's departure (111-113), which is treated by our bard as synchronous with the eclipse (114-119), cannot be separated from Igor's speech during that eclipse by the apostrophe to Boyan. The section corresponding to my 91-110 seems to have filled exactly one page in the original, and this page might have got accidentally transferred from after page 5 to after page 3.

52   Of the times of old: *starago vremeni.* Cf. Macpherson's *Fingal,* Book II (p. 81, vol. I, Laing's edition of *The Poems of Ossian,* Edinburgh, 1805): "To the ages of old, to the days of other years"; and "Carthon," first line (p. 311, vol. I, Laing's edition): "A tale of the times of old! The deeds of days of other years!"

It is from French versions of "Ossian," not from The Song (which at that time he did not know as well as he did later) that young Pushkin borrowed the lines relating to *his* Boyan (borrowed from Heraskov) in "Ruslan and Ludmila" (1820):

Delá davnó minúvshih dnéy,
Predán'ya stariní glubókoy. . .

The deeds of days past long ago,
traditions of deep ancientry. . . .

line

54-55   Hopping, O nightingale, over (i.e., upon and about) the tree of thought ("cogitational tree"), *skacha slaviyu po mïslenu drevu*. As if in compensation for the absence, nominally, of the first emblematic animal at 14, now the nightingale is present, but the rest of the trio, the eagle and wolf, are not named.

56-57   (See also lines 13 and 17-18.) A similar image (possibly implying a knowledge of The Song), *parya mïsliyu aki orel po vozduhu*, soaring in thought as the eagle upon the air, is found in the remarkable *Molenie Daniila Zatochnika*, Lament of Daniel the Confined—a native of Pereyaslavl (early thirteenth century). This is a resonant plea of considerable poetical merit voiced by a young man in trouble who after accumulating all sorts of biblical and local metaphors ends with a series of colorful allusions to such exploits as reckless riding in the hippodrome or flying from the church tops by means of silken wings. He is said to have been banished to a remote lake shore in the Olonets region.

59   Roving the Troyan trail: *rishcha v tropu Troyanyu*. What is this trail or path which is being reached, or penetrated by a poet racing, wolflike, across country? Its punning correspondence to *"Tropaeum Traiani,"* Trojan's Trophy, a monument to the Roman emperor Marcus Ulpius Nerva Trajanus (52-117 of our era) erected at the beginning of the second century in Dobrujia, cannot be dismissed as a mere coincidence. It may be the obscure echo of a foreign name.

"Trajan's roads" are known to have existed in various parts of the Black Sea region. On the other hand, a god called Troyan, attributes and functions unknown, is mentioned in a twelfth century transcript of one of the apocrypha relating to the activities of the Blessed Virgin (*Hozhdenie Bogoroditsï po Mukam*) where he heads a company of condemned idols: "Troyan, Hors, Veles, Perun." (The last is the god of thunder, and the two others are Hors, the sun god, and Veles, the god of shepherds, the Russian Apollo). The Roman emperor and the Russian god seem to have got hopelessly entangled by the time The Song was composed. One can understand line 59 as "following the divine way (of inspiration and magic?)," or endow it with a geographical sense (in connection with line 307). The mysterious Troyan is mentioned four times in The Song, the other three references being: 231, "There have been the ages of Troyan," *Bïli vyechi Troyani;* 307, "into Troyan's land," *na zemlyu Troyanyu;* and 631, "In the seventh age of Troyan," *na sed'mom vyetsye Troyani.* At 231 the meaning is, presumably, "heathen times" (Karamzin says that the word in the MS was not *vyechi* but *syechi,* "battles," but we have to follow the *editio princeps*). At 304-310 there is the image of Wrong, the Anti-virgin, entering southern Russia (a region metaphysically ruled by the legendary amalgam evoked at 59). Finally, at 631, in reference to Vseslav's adventure in the year 1068, the "seventh age" would seem to relate to the centuries elapsed since the fall of Roman rule in the Kievan region.

line

63   A type of construction (negative metaphor) much used in Russian folklore; "it is not a storm that has swept falcons . . .": *Ne burya sokoli zanese . . .*

66   Grandson of Veles: *Velesov' vnuche.* "Grandson" in the general sense of descendant, scion, the archaic "nephew," Latin *nepos,* the *neveu* of French pseudoclassicism. A footnote on p. 7 of the *editio princeps* says "Veles, a Slavic God [*sic*] in heathendom, the protector of herds. . . ." Veles, or Volos (perhaps akin to Helios) is mentioned by the chronicles as being the god of cattle. The invocation *Velesov vnuche* bears an odd resemblance to the pseudoclassical *neveu d'Apollon.* The Song mentions four other known pagan gods: Stribog, the god of winds (197); Dazhbog, or Dazhdbog, the god of abundance (258, 305); Hors, (Horus), the god of the rising sun (665); and Troyan (59, 231, 307, 631). Our bard ignores Perun, the Russian Jupiter, whose effigy Vladimir I caused to be drowned in the Dnepr. Instead of him, the Christian deity (perhaps, substituted by a scribe for Stribog) amiably directs events in one passage, and one passage only (733).

67   The Sula is the frontier river, or one of the frontier rivers, east of Kiev, beyond which spreads the Kuman-infested steppe (see Map). So great is our bard's preoccupation with the Sula (67, 123, 563, 583) that one can hardly help locating his home in that region—perhaps, in Pereyaslavl. Novgorod-Seversk and Putivl mentioned further are the seats of Igor and his son Vladimir.

line

1-70   Under the pretext of trying to decide what style to adopt, the old, involved, and grandiloquent style of Boyan, or something more in keeping with a contemporaneous subject—the would-be singer of Igor's campaign asks himself how would Boyan have begun, invents examples of Boyan's poetical idiom (63-70), as if to see how they fit recent events, toys with them, rejects them—but in the meantime he has craftily and successfully fashioned of them the beginning of his story. Thus, in his *Pamyatnik* (The Monument), Pushkin in 1836 parodied a poem by his predecessor Derzhavin (1743-1816) on a Horatian theme (*"Exegi monumentum . . ."*), in order to smuggle in his own secret aspirations, his own secret pride, under the cloak of high mummery.

71   Art and history are at variance in this passage and in the next ones. Our bard has Igor await Vsevolod (who is presumably coming from Trubchevsk which lies 50 miles to the north) at Novgorod-Seversk, the starting point of the general march east; and in order to enhance the dramatic force of the portent, he has further, at 91-116, the solar eclipse (which historically took place on May 1) coincide with Igor's setting out from Novgorod-Seversk (which historically took place on April 23). Vsevolod's speech concerning his forces—already collected ahead near Kursk—is likewise synchronized with an eclipse which is not over when, at 111-114, Igor rides out into the prairie. The Ipatiev Chronicle, on the other hand, implies that after starting on their march from Novgorod-

line

Seversk on Tuesday, April 23, 1185, the brothers separated somewhere on the way (near Putivl or near Rïlsk), Vsevolod heading for a point just south of Kursk to place himself at the head of his militia, and Igor proceeding slowly toward the Donets. On May 1, as he was reaching that river, the historical Igor witnessed the eclipse and according to the chronicles made a long speech to his retinue, upon which he at once forded the Donets, reached the Oskol watershed, and for a couple of days waited there for Vsevolod who (still according to the chronicles) was coming by another route, from the Kursk area, about 100 miles north. It is curious to note that the Lavrentiev Chronicle (which is not considered reliable in respect of places and dates) has Igor start not from Novgorod-Seversk but from Pereyaslavl (where perhaps our Song started), with *two* sons, besides his brother and nephew.

72   The names *Buy Tur*, Wild Bull or Turbulent Aurochs, and *Yar Tur*, Fierce Bull or Ardent Aurochs, as applied to Vsevolod have struck nonbelievers in the authenticity of The Song as Americanisms of the late eighteenth century imported into Russia via France. *Tur* may mean either of the two species of *Bos*, the real *tur*, urus, *Bos primigenus* (from which the domestic ox has been evolved) and the *zubr*, aurochs, *Bison bonasus*. By the twelfth century the primigenial bull was extinct but aurochs occurred in southern Russia up to the eighteenth century and symbolized courage and strength. On the other hand, the word

line

tur has consistently been applied in the Ukraine to a large gray form of domestic bull.

73   One brother: *odin brat.* As Szeftel notes (in *La Geste du Prince Igor,* p. 103), Igor's eldest brother, Oleg (father of Svyatoslav of Rïlsk), from whom he had inherited his princedom of Novgorod-Seversk, had been dead for at least five years.

83   Ravines: *yarugi.* The comparatively rare word *yaruga.* which in our times is still a regional term for the northern *ovrag* or the southern *balka* (meaning "gully," "hollow," "barranca," and so forth), occurs three times in The Song (83, 134, and 362).

91   As mentioned in the note to lines 51-70, the following section probably represents one misplaced page of the lost original (in the First Edition and in the Apograph this passage comes between the sentences rendered by my lines 50 and 53). The solar eclipse— that blinking eye of Clio—started at 3:25 P.M., Wednesday, May 1, 1185, when the historical Igor was approaching the Donets after a week's march from Novgorod-Seversk. The Ipatiev Chronicle describes the eclipse in terms that bear a singular resemblance to those of The Song, with which the chronicler may have been familiar (to mention only one possibility); but the pious and didactic speech which the historical Igor makes to his warriors lacks the poetical eloquence, aphoristic conciseness, and sportive zest of the corresponding passage (95-100)

line

in The Song; both addresses are marked by a fatalistic strain but the wording is different except for a bizarre coincidence of terms at the start. Here is the relevant passage in the Ipatiev Chronicle: "Igor glanced up at the sky [cf. line 91], and saw the sun standing moonlike, and said to his boyars and his Guards: 'Do you know what that is?' Whereupon they gazed and saw all, and their heads drooped, and the men said: 'Prince! This omen bodes no good [cf. end of the King's Dream].' And Igor said: 'Brothers and Guards [cf. 95]! None knows the secrets of God,'" etc. The Lavrentiev Chronicle supplies the following highly artistic description of the eclipse: "On May 1 [1185] there was an eclipse of the sun, in the afternoon; for more than an hour it was most murky; the stars were visible, as if it were night, and people saw green [*voochiyu zeleno byashe*], and the sun dwindled to what seemed a moon crescent, from whose horns there seemed to issue a glowing ember [or "burning coal," *ugl' goryashch'*]."

94-95   The Guard, the Guards: *druzhina;* retinue, bodyguard, a company of knights under the direct leadership of the territorial ruler.

100   Blue. The epithet as applied to the river Don here, and to the sea further on, is a mere cliché of folklore eloquence. It is not, or is no longer, a color epithet in the specific visual sense, and thus should not be confused with the livid flash of the blue lightnings at 187, or with the dark amethyst of the blue wine at 397.

line

108   *Rusitsi* or *Rusichi:* here and elsewhere (148, 209) our bard employs this nonce word as an affectionate form of address (*Rus'* being transformed into a kind of tender patronymic).

110   A formula found also in the chronicles: "Formerly Vladimir Monomachus drank from his golden helmet the Don" (Ipatiev Chronicle, 1201).

112   The formula is repeated at 237.

115-117   The sudden night due to the eclipse causes the nocturnal birds of prey to awake and the bobacs (marmots) and susliks (ground squirrels) to utter warning whistles. This passage is badly disfigured and the meaning is problematic. Line 117 (*svist zvyerin v sta*) and the continuation of the last word commencing the next line (*zbi*) are missing in the Apograph.

118-126   The Daeva, or Diva, *Div* is the demon bird of Oriental myths, a cross between an owl and a peacock. It is here an agent of the Kumans and will swoop down from the top of his poplar at 443. Something of the kind occurs in *Ossian*. Lines 9-10 in Macpherson's "First Bard" (in "The Six Bards, a Fragment," see vol. II, pp. 416-417 of Laing's edition) read in their "verse for verse" form:

> From the tree at the grave of the dead
> The lonely screech-owl groans.

line

which in the "measured prose" form become "From the tree at the grave of the dead the long-howling owl is heard." This is rendered by Letourneur (*Ossian, fils de Fingal, barde du III siècle: Poésies Galliques,* Paris, 1777, two volumes) as "*La chouette glapissante crie au haut de l'arbre qui est auprès de la tombe des morts.*"

120   The steppes to the south and to the east of the river Sula, where the Kumans roam, are termed "the land unknown" or (276, 516) "field unknown." The Daeva's command "to the land unknown," *zemli nez-naemye,* is to take heed, *poslushati.* Cf. in "The War of Inis-thona" (vol. I, Laing's edition, p. 264), "The traveller is sad in a land unknown"; also, in "Cath-loda" (*op. cit.* vol. II, p. 298 and p. 318), "Few are the heroes of Morven, in a land unknown!" and, "He fell pale, in a land unknown." The Russian counterpart "*zemlya neznaema*" frequently occurs in the chronicles (for example, under the year 1093; see Lihachyov, in the Andrianov-Peretts edition, p. 394). Letourneur (1777) who never renders, of course, the intonations, the mournful cut, the pathetic brevity of Macpherson, translates the first "Cath-loda" passage thus: "*Les héros de Morven ne descendirent pas en grand nombre sur cette terre inconnue.*"

124-125   Surozh (Sudak) and Korsun (Hersones, Chersonesus, a Greek colony) are Crimean place names, and from that peninsula, in lines 444-449, Goth maidens will presently echo the Daeva's cry.

line

126   *Tmutorokan'* was in the region of the present Taman, on the Sea of Surozh (now Sea of Azov). This fiercely coveted town had been a Russian princedom in the eleventh century, and its loss to the Kumans rankled badly, especially in the mind of Igor to whose grandfather Oleg it had belonged. The "idol" presumably refers to some huge Greek statue, such as that of Astarte or Artemis, which had been erected there in the third century B.C.

127   Untrodden: *negotovami.* With a sense of "unprepared."

128   Here and at 178-180, commentators disagree as to the direction in which the Kumans move *(pobyegosha* may mean "flee" as well as "run" or "speed")— retiring eastward to the Don from their places of hibernation in the Donets Basin, or on the contrary hurrying westward to the Don from the Volga region in order to repulse the Russians. The former seems to be the better sense, especially in conjunction with the image of the disturbed swans at 130, and with the general theme of cunning enticement and foolhardy pursuit adumbrated throughout the next sections up to the ominous passage 203-204 when the Kumans attack the Russians who have advanced too far. There is no need to take into account a sentence in the blundering Lavrentiev Chronicle which has the Kumans proclaim that they will "march against them (the Russians) beyond the Don," i.e., from east to west.

line

130   The allusion is to the mournful, clarinet-like cry of migrating flocks of swans, a characteristic feature of spring nights on the lakes and marshes of southern Russia.

131   Donward: *k Donu.* Igor proceeds in a general south-easterly direction, through the brush which grades into grass prairie between the Donets and the Oskol (see Map).

133   In the oakscrub, in the chaparral. I accept the reading *po dubiyu,* instead of the *podobiyu* of the text.

139   Vermilion shields: *chorleniya shchiti;* modern Russian: *chervlyonïe shchiti.* The Russian shields of the time were ovate in form, manufactured of light wood, rimmed with iron, and painted a bright carmine red by means of *cherlen',* a color made of *chervets* ("little worm," *"vermiculus"* specifically the scale insect *Coccus polonicus*) which is not as deep as kermes (rich crimson, Russian *bagrets*). Vermilion as applied to chemical dyes has lost today the rosy tinge it formerly had.

141   Behind the culmen, beyond the culm, or helm (in the sense of hill): *za shelomyanem.* It has been conjectured that in The Song this Shelomya, or Sholomya, is a definite place, namely the Izyum Tumulus in the Donets region; which would abolish the poetry.

line

151   According to the chronicler, the historical Igor met the
       army of the Kumans Friday morning (May 10) on the
       west bank of the lost river Syuurliy (apparently a trib-
       utary of the Donets south of the Oskol). After shoot-
       ing from the opposite bank a first hurtle of arrows, the
       Kumans fled into the prairie. The Russians pursued
       them and captured the tents they had left behind.

162-163 Plankings to plank: *mostï mostiti*, grammatically,
         "[with] bridges to bridge"; the allusion is to cause-
         ways laid across marshy ground.

165   Possibly this phrase, which is preceded by an "and"
       in the text, begins a new sentence, the rest of which
       is lost. Some editors in order to keep the conjunction
       transfer "and with all kinds of Kuman weaves" to a
       position between 161 and 162.

172   The reference is to the descendants of Oleg of
       Tmutorokan (d. 1115), dubbed Malglory (*Gorislavich*),
       son of Svyatoslav II, brother of Roman of Tmutorokan,
       grandson of Yaroslav I and grandfather of Svyatoslav III
       as well as of Igor. See in this respect the uniquely impor-
       tant passage 255-260. The Lavrentiev Chronicle starts
       its brief account of Igor's campaign with the words:
       "Oleg's grandsons bethought themselves of setting out
       against the Kumans to obtain praise for themselves."

178   Khan Gzak (Gza, Kza, Koza) seems to have been the
       father of the Kuman chieftain who was to capture
       Vladimir, Igor's son (see note 8 to Foreword).

line

179   With his present foe Konchak, and with another Than (Kobyaka, see note to 365-369), the historical Igor had formed some five years before a brief alliance in his feud with the sons of Rostislav I, and together they suffered an ignominious defeat at Dolobsk, in 1180. Igor and Konchak jumped into a boat and barely escaped capture. Although, after this, Igor broke with the Kumans, he was not invited to take part in the campaign which his cousin Svyatoslav III successfully waged against Kobyaka.

182   Bloody effulgences: *krovavïya zori*. The turn is clumsy and I would have said (needing a plural form) "blood-red auroras," bur *zori* is used in Russian for the glow of both rising and setting sun. See also 284, *pred zoryami*, before the (plural) glow (of sunrise).

186   The four Russian leaders, Igor of Novgorod-Seversk, his son, Vladimir of Putivl, his brother Vsevolod of Kursk, and their nephew, Svyatoslav of Rïlsk.

187   Blue lightnings. Our bard is far ahead of his first editor's time. The blue throb of an electric discharge is a modern conception. Most people with some amount of color sense today see lightning as a flash of ozone blue. Writers of the eighteenth and early nineteenth centuries rationalized whatever impact lightning had on their sluggish retinas as "yellow" or "red" because logic told them that this was the color of fire. Macpherson has "the red lightning of heaven" in *Fingal*, Book IV (vol. I, Laing's edition, p. 131)

line

and Pushkin has "with the red glitter," *bleskom alïm*, of lightning in a short poem ("The Tempest," 1825). We also find in Macpherson's "Oithona" (vol. I, p. 527) the "red path of lightning on a stormy cloud"; but on the other hand, there is also "thy sword is before thee, a blue fire of night," steel being blue (Macpherson's footnote to *Temora*, Book VI, vol. II, p. 179). It is curious to note that the first commentators of The Song could not understand why the lightnings were "blue." Musin and his assistants translate the original phrase *v nih trepeshchut sinii molnii* into routine eighteenth century Russian as *sverkaet v nih molniya*, "lightning flashes in them."

194   Today the bed of the stream cannot be located exactly. The Kayala is supposed to have emptied in the Surozh Sea (Azov Sea) after traversing Kuman country. There I have marked it on the Map. A punning twist is given to its name in later passages.

196   See note to 141.

197   Stribog, the Slavic god of the Wind. The annals for A.D. 980 list the idols "wooden Perun, with a head of silver and a mustache of gold; Dazhbog, and Stribog, and Simar'gla, and Mokosha," Perun is the god of thunder, and Dazhbog (see 258 and 305), the god of fertility. The two others are unknown.

200-202   The cavalry muddies the rivers at fords, makes the earth reverberate and causes clouds of dust to veil the plain.

line

206   Modern editors prefer to read *ostupisha* (surround) instead of *otstupisha* (retreat, as in the First Edition and in the Apograph), and to connect the preceding words "and from all sides" with the Kumans (as in lines 322-323) who "surround the Russian troops." I see no reason for this manipulation, even though in other manuscripts, such as the chronicles, early transcribers are known to have confused the two words.

207   The children of the devil: *dyeti byesovi*. The Ipatiev Chronicle supplies the name of these Kuman chieftains. They are reeled off by Igor in a curse-spitting speech before the Saturday battle: "Konchak, and Kza, and Toksobich, and Kolobich, and Etebich, and Tetrobich" (the last four are apparently patronymics).

211-230   The Ipatiev Chronicle says that they, the Russians, "fought on foot, and in their midst Vsevolod showed no little valor." Igor was wounded in the left hand or arm, and was on horseback.

214-215,   *Gremleshi o shelomi mechi haraluzhnïmi . . . poskepani . . .*
219-220   *shelomi*, you clang on helmets with sword of steel . . . cleft are helmets. Cf. *Fingal*, Book I (pp. 34-35, Laing's edition of *The Poems of Ossian*, vol. I): "Steel, clanging, sounds on steel. Helmets are cleft on high." *Haraluzhnïy* is supposed to mean "made of steel," "steely." In the *Zadonshchina* it seems to be used as a synonym of *bulatnïy* (the ordinary adjective for weapons of steel) but also as an epithet of river banks which The Song calls "silver." The derivation of *haraluzhnïy* has

line

been sought in the Turkish language and in old Russian allusions to Charlemagne, Carolus Magnus, which would turn it into "Frankish steel."

217   *Svoim zlatïm shelomom posvyechivaya.* The effect of this image on the mind of the reader is curiously similar to that of "Intermitting, darts the light from his shield" in Macpherson's *Temora*, Book V (p. 149, vol. II, of Laing's edition). The phrase is also found in the *Zadonshchina* where it appears as *zlatïm shelomom posvyechivashe*, and other variants such as *dospye-hom* (armor) instead of *shelomom* (helmet).

220   The Avars were a Caucasian tribe. The kind of helmet they made (in Daghestan, East Caucasus) had a sharp apical point and a spatulate neck guard.

228-229   Of his dear beloved, Gleb's fair daughter: *svoya milïya hoti krasnïya Glyebovni:* The reference is presumably to Olga, daughter of Gleb of Pereyaslavl (d. 1171), son of Yuriy of Suzdal and grandson of Vladimir II (founder of the House of Monomachus).

230   *Svïchaya i obïchaya.* A taglike formula meaning "love and endearments" or "devotion and affection."

231-250   The intonation of the first line here resembles the apostrophe to Boyan (51-70), while on the other hand, the invocation of Oleg's feuds prepares the magnificent apostrophizations of the 471-650 section. For Troyan see note to 59.

line

232, 241   The references are to Yaroslav I (see note to 25), his son Svyatoslav II (d. 1076), and his grandson Oleg of Tmutorokan.

242-244   Vladimir II (d. 1125), known as Vladimir Monomachus, son of Vsevolod I, grandson of Yaroslav I and first cousin of Oleg of Tmutorokan, Igor's grandfather. He is the author of a remarkable *Pouchenie* (Testament).

245-250   Boris (d. 1078), son of Vyacheslav of Smolensk and grandson of Yaroslav I. He was slain fighting his uncles Izyaslav and Vsevolod in the battle of Nezhatina Niva, near Chernigov (where there existed, as a tributary of the Desna, a small Kanin stream, mentioned in relation to another prince by the chronicle of 1152). Boris in his pride had dismissed the prudent advice to surrender given him by his ally Oleg Malglory, Igor's grandfather. The "green pall" seems to be a metaphorical allusion to the rank weeds of the unharvested plain growing over the bodies of the dead warriors. Some commentators apply the concluding clause (250) to Boris rather than to Oleg.

251   A kind of metaphorical pun is intended here. The Kanin river (247) was the site of calamities similar to those connected with the Kayala river, and the latter name, although of non-Russian origin (possibly, as has been suggested, from Kayalï, meaning in Turkish "canyon-like" or "rocky," and identified by some as applicable to the Kalmius, flowing into the Azov Sea) has in Russian the connotation of "lament," "regret," "reproach." See also note to 292.

line

252   Svyatopolk II (d. 1113), son of Izyaslav I (d. 1078), grandson of Yaroslav I, and first cousin of Oleg Malglory. His father was killed in the same battle as Boris (see preceding note). The two amblers, both bestridden, were hitched one behind the other, with the litter between gently lolling to the rhythm of their pace. It is curious that the Kievan chronicle mentions another church, not St. Sophia, as Izyaslav's burying place, but our bard, not the chronicler, is right, as confirmed by a text in the "First Sophian annals," published by Kudryavtsev only recently (1925).

255-260   *Togda pri Olzye Gorislavlichi syeyashetsya i rastyashet' usobitsami; pogibashet' zhizn' Dazhd'-Bozha vnuka, v Knyazhih kramolah vyetsi chelovyekom' skratishas'.* Thus in the First Edition, pp. 16-17. The Apograph has *"pogibashet',"* *"knyashih,"* and *"chelovyekom."* This passage has the unique distinction of having been paraphrased in another work—not the *Zadonshchina.* A learned monk writes at the end of the Pskovan *Apostol* of 1307 (these Acts of the Apostles, dated 1307 and 1309-1312 came from the Monastery of St. Panteleymon near Pskov), in reference to the struggle between two princes of the time, Yuriy of Moscow and Mihail of Tver: *"Pri sih knyazeh syeyashetsya i rostyashe usobitsami; ginyashe zhizn' nasha v knyazyeh kotorï, i vyetsi skorotishasya chelovyekom"* ("under these princes sown were and grew discords, perished our livelihood in princely quarrels, and human ages [i.e., lives] dwindled"). He substitutes a pronoun for the pagan phrase applied by our bard to the Russian

line

people "grandson of Dazh[d]bog," in which "grandson" (*vnuk*, Latin *nepos*) is used collectively, and Dazhbog is the ancient god of fertility and abundance.

269-270   Our bard greatly exaggerates the scope and significance of this affray.

273-275   A similar din of arms is heard in "Berrathon" (p. 566, vol. I, of Laing's edition): "Darts hiss through the air. Spears ring on mails. Swords on broken bucklers bound." This is immediately followed in The Song (276) by the very Ossianic "in the field unknown" (see note to 120).

276-281   A sustained tilling metaphor of which other examples are found further.

282-283   *Chto mi shumit', chto mi zvenit'?* The wistful and tuneful intonation of this lyrical phrase cannot be rendered in literal translation. The natural rhyme in this passage of the basically rhymeless Song is the result—a not unusual one in immemorial folk songs—of a coincidence of simple verbal endings. In the history of European rhyme the first words to mate were verbs. Cf. *Igor spit, Igor bdit* at 738-739.

285   The Ipatiev Chronicle for the year 1185 relates that the *kovui* (Turkic mercenaries, a company of which, under one Olstin, had been given to Igor by his cousin Yaroslav of Chernigov) were the first to be put to rout. Igor, who by then was wounded, rode out to them to make them return. In this he failed,

line

and on his way back to his regiment was taken prisoner by a Kuman chieftain (Chilbuk). As he was being tied and borne away, he could see his brother Vsevolod still fighting desperately.

287-290   A recapitulation; the triple formula—otherwise a stock device of all epics—reflects here the actual sequence of events. The chronicle says the battle, including the first skirmish, lasted all Friday, continued Saturday and ended Sunday.

292   Kudryashov identifies it with the river Makatiha in the region of the Tor salt lakes (where the mercenaries drowned).

296   In-laws: *svati*. Russian princes often married Kuman girls; these were renowned for their beauty. Our bard is evidently aware at the time of writing that Igor's son is to wed, or has actually wed, in captivity Konchak's daughter. Igor's grandfather, Oleg, had married the daughter of a Khan Asalup, and Igor's stepmother was the granddaughter of a Khan Girgen. There is thus a specific slant to the sustained metaphor of the feast illustrating the battle.

299-301   See also 387-390, 611-614, 801-802.

303   *Uzhe pustïni silu prikrila.* The image is that of the prairie grass concealing the dead heroes (see 248).

305   See 258.

line

306-310   As pointed out by various commentators, the image of a swanlike maiden personifying Bodement, Calamity or Injustice, is an ancient component of Russian folklore.

330   This bizarre expression of grief is attested by an ancient miniature illustrating funeral rites of 1096, in the Chronicle of Radzivill, first reproduced in 1902 (see *La Geste du Prince Igor,* p. 190).

333   Our dear husbands: *svoih milih lad; lada:* darling, spouse, consort of either sex (the word is also used at 703, 717 and 725).

345-350   This is a very artistic repetition and development of the theme at 320-323.

349   *Belya,* a vair skin; *belaya veveritsa,* white sable, or more probably blue-gray squirrel, dearer of course than ordinary squirrel, one skin of which would not have been much of a tax.

351-357   Here our bard expresses his basic political views (further reflected in 455-465 and 479-482) as he pronounces a severe judgment on Igor.

356   Svyatoslav III (d. 1194) son of Vsevolod II and grandson of Oleg Malglory, thus Igor's first cousin. His actual dominion was limited to the city of Kiev, the rest of the Kievan region being ruled by Rurik, son of Rostislav I (House of Mstislav), with whom he

line

had routed the Kumans in 1183, without Igor's participation. The remarkable passage devoted to his dream (391-405) is being prepared by our bard.

365, 369 Kobyaka, a Kuman khan with whom Igor had been in a brief alliance (see note to 179).

366 *Iz luka morya.* The allusion is to the bend of the Azov Sea at the mouth of the Don. In the Lavrentiev Chronicle the Kumans are made to say *"Idyom po nih u luku morya"* (Let us go along the bight of the sea to get them).

387-390 *Unisha bo . . . zabrali, a veselie poniche:* mournful are the ramparts, merriment has drooped. Cf. in *The Poems of Ossian*, "The Death of Cuthullin" (p. 369, vol. I, of Laing's edition): "Mournful are Tura's walls. Sorrow dwells at Dunscäi."

Zabrali means more exactly the breastwork set up on the ramparts of fortified towns to protect their defenders. It is also there that Euphrosyne mourns in the section 691-730.

397 *Sinee vino:* blue wine. The allusion is either to whortleberry wine or dark grape wine. One recalls that the Greeks saw the dark-blue sea as wine-colored (for the interpretation of which there is no need to drag in a reflected sunset as some color-blind Homerians do). A very dark red wine does have a purple-blue depth of tone like the southern seas—especially in warm patches near the coast. In fact, I would have said "purple wine" had not the epithet almost turned to blood-red under

line

the influence of Continental, especially French, concepts of *pourpre*. In this connection it is amusing to note that Russians translate the purple of English poets as applied to the sea as *purpurnoe* (or *bagryanoe*), which, as in French, is crimson, instead of the correct *lilovo-sinee* or *fioletovoe*. According to a footnote on page 185, vol. I, of Laing's edition of *Ossian (Fingal,* Book VI), the Caledonians used a liquor which they called "blue water" (said to be *"Gorm-ui"* in Erse), and this no doubt was a bilberry wine.

398-400   Cp. with the old Oriental and Spanish custom of marking one's glad days with white pebbles and one's sad days with black ones. A dying man might like to have the boxful of his days sorted out to measure how happy he had been. We may imagine a warrior king using a quiver for a box and pearls for his days of triumph. One also thinks of Tamerlane (Tamburlaine, Timur Leng, Mongol emperor of the fourteenth century), who in the dust and terror of fabulous marches had each soldier, on the way to battle, lay down a stone and remove one on the way back, so that the mound left by the survivors automatically served as a monument to the fallen.

The tulks are tame heathens, domesticated aliens, used as interpreters.

407   Demon ravens, *bosuvi vrani.* The translation of the adjective is conjectural. I have followed those scholars who distinguish a connection between it and the equally obscure epithets at 448 (demon times, *vremya*

line

Busovo, see note) and at 757 (demon wolf, *bosïm volkom*). Cf. also the *dyeti byesovï* at 207. Other commentators have suggested that all three epithets (407, 448, 757) should be simply translated by "dusky" (for which there is an old Russian word *busïy*); but this would be a very artificial color epithet for the raven and the wolf which have their traditional "black" and "gray," respectively, firmly attached to them by stylistic tradition (see, for example, 176 and 15).

408-410　　The passage is very corrupt and it is not clear why the town of Plesensk (see Map) should provide the sleigh (it has also been suggested that the name may stand for Plosk, implying a *ploskaya chast'*, flat part near Kiev). An illustration to a Lives of Saints MS of the fourteenth century, showing four men carrying a boat-shaped logging sleigh with a corpse to be buried, seems to explain nicely the image here; and the sea is the burial place of the great.

415-416　　This sounds as if the boyars were ironically quoting Igor (see 110), the foolish and flighty prince. Tmutorokan (Greek Tamatarakha)—a rich town and region on the Taman peninsula—had belonged to Russia in the eleventh century and was usually the princedom of Chernigov rulers. Igor, as other princes before him, dreamt of getting it back from the Kumans.

424-430　　Cf. *Fingal*, Book V (Laing's edition, vol. I, p. 174): "they sunk behind the hill, like two pillars of the fire of night." Who are the "both young moons," *molodaya*

line

myesyatsa? The names Oleg and Svyatoslav which follow may either apply to the second and third sons of Igor (both of them mere children), or else "Oleg" may have been a scribe's substitution for Vladimir (Igor's eldest son, 1173-1212), and then "Svyatoslav" should mean the young prince of Rïlsk (1166-1186), Igor's nephew whose patronymic (Oleg) perhaps influenced the slip. The chronicles do not tell us if Igor had taken his two younger sons with him in the 1185 campaign; but they do tell us that in 1183 Igor summoned his son Oleg, aged nine (or rather the company of knights under Oleg's nominal leadership), besides Svyatoslav of Rïlsk and Vsevolod of Kursk, to fight the Kumans who that time evaded battle (see also note to 71). As to 430, this phrase is obviously misplaced in the text, jammed as it is between 435 and 436, where it makes no sense. Historically nobody was drowned except the unfortunate mercenaries who perished in one of the lakes of the Tor, termed in the chronicle a "sea." The two setting suns are certainly Igor and Vsevolod. Their red columniformed reflections in the water (a fine metaphor based on exact observation) are either their retinues or (if we accept the meaning of the two moons as Igor's younger sons) they represent the two other leaders, Svyatoslav of Rïlsk and Vladimir of Putivl.

We are at the mid-point of The Song.

Opinions vary as to whether the passage 422-430 is a continuation of the boyars' speech or, as I think it is, an authorial interpolation after which the courtiers and counselors take over again.

line

437   Imparted to the Hin: *podast' Hinovï*. The name, a
nonce word, probably applies to the entire group of
Asiatic tribes as known to the Russians (see further
555 and 701).

442   See note to 118-126.

444   A Teutonic tribe in the Crimea, remnants of the East
Goths, vanquished by the Huns and sympathetic to
the Kumans.

448   *Vremya Busovo*. See note to 407. It has also been suggested that the reference is to an ancient king of the
Antes, Bos, Bous, or Booz, who was defeated by a
king of the Goths in the fourth century.

449   Sharokan, spelled also Sharohan or Sharukan, a
Kuman chief, Konchak's grandfather who had been
defeated by the Russians in a great battle on the Sula
river in 1107.

450   Guards: *druzhina*. I suppose this is here a synonym
for "boyars," though the actual meaning, of course,
is retinue, bodyguard, etc.

453   In regard to the historical Svyatoslav III and the
events of 6693 (=1185 A.D.), as described in the
annals, nothing is said about his seeing a prophetic
dream at the time; but at one point the Ipatiev
Chronicle does briefly coincide with The Song.
When in Chernigov (not Kiev) late in May, 1185,

line

Svyatoslav was informed by one Byelovolod of the defeat of Igor, he "wiped his tears and said . . ." The little speech of 46 words which follows (with Svyatoslav both pitying Igor and regretting that by his rashness Igor had destroyed the results of his, Svyatoslav's, former victory) is not textually paralleled in The Song except for a reference to the Pagans "throwing open the gates to the Russian land," a phrase in the chronicle which resembles 528, 533 and 647 insofar as *vorota* (gates) are mentioned.

456-457　Cf. *Fingal*, Book III (vol. I, p. 90, Laing's edition): "Early were thy deeds in arms."

470　Yaroslav of Chernigov (d. 1198), son of Vsevolod II and brother of Svyatoslav III. Historically he did supply Igor with a regiment of mercenaries.

Cf. the intonation of this passage with *Temora*, Book I (p. 19, vol. II, of Laing's edition): "Cathmor, my brother, is not here. He is not here with his thousands."

472-474　A list of the tribal names or nicknames of mercenary troops. None has been identified with complete certainty although some suggest obvious determinations to tempt the scholiast.

492　Rim or Rimov, a town on the Sula, was sacked by the Kumans on their way back from Pereyaslavl. See next note.

line

494-496 Volodimir or Vladimir of Pereyaslavl, son of Gleb of Ryazan. It would seem that the rumors of his death in result of the wounding blows had not yet reached our bard, and this helps us to date The Song rather accurately (see note 12 to Foreword). In the summer or autumn of 1185, after defeating Igor, Konchak, proceeding westward, tried to storm Pereyaslavl but was repelled by its prince, Volodimir. The latter was badly wounded; nonetheless he marched against the Kumans (who by then had taken Rim). He returned to Pereyaslavl very ill, and died there on April 18, 1187. The news of his death should not have taken more than a fortnight to reach our bard, if he was anywhere in the Kiev region.

497 Vsevolod of Vladimir (a town in the Suzdal region), later Vsevolod III (d. 1212), surnamed The Big Nest, son of Yuriy I. In Igor's time this Vsevolod was perhaps the most powerful prince among the descendants of Vladimir Monomachus, his grandfather.

500-501 In 1183 Vsevolod had overcome the Volga Bulgarians (Bolgars) and sunk a number of their vessels.

504-508 The general meaning of this passage is that "if *you* were here, fighting the Kumans, your prisoners would be so numerous that their price on the crowded slave market would become ridiculously small." One nogata was the twentieth part of a grivna which consisted of fifty rezanas. The average price of a male slave at the time was five grivnas (a hundred

line

nogatas or two hundred and fifty rezanas). In terms of hides, a rezana or ryazana was a cut skin worth twenty kopeks, and a nogata was a whole skin, including the feet, worth fifty kopeks.

509   Bolts: *shereshiri*. The meaning of the word is not quite settled. Some form of "Greek fire" may be implied. Curiously, the epithet "live" (*zhivïmi*) is lacking in the Apograph.

510   The "brave sons of Gleb" are the four brothers of Volodimir of Pereyaslavl.

511-518   Rurik of Belgorod (d. 1215), a mighty prince, and David of Smolensk (d. 1198), sons of Rostislav I (d. 1168) and grandsons of Mstislav I (d. 1132). A third brother, Mstislav of Smolensk (d. 1180), is mentioned patronymically at 572. Turbulent Igor had feuded with these princes some seven years before The Song was composed. The "floating on blood" presumably alludes to a battle with the Kumans fought by Rurik and David in 1183, on the river Orel, or Horol.

523-539   Yaroslav of Galich, surnamed Osmomïsl (of the Eight Thoughts). He was the father of Igor's wife, Euphrosyne. He died on October 1, 1187, a few months after being addressed by our bard.

529   The word in the First Edition and in the Apograph is *vremeni*, which all commentators read as *bremeni*, weights; perhaps, heavy stones shot from catapults.

line

535   This is thought to be an allusion to a possible partic-
      ipation of the Galich warriors in the Third Crusade.

538   Slave: *kashchey*, in the sense of "villain."

542-559   Two princes of the Mstislav House: Roman of
          Galich, son of Mstislav II, a great warrior and a cel-
          ebrated prince, killed in a battle with the Poles in
          1205; and Mstislav of Peresopnits (d. 1224), son of
          Yaroslav of Lutsk, whose two other sons are men-
          tioned at 571.

551   Breastplates: *paporzi*. This nonce word has been
      associated by Buslaev with *"persi,"* breast, and by
      Peretts with *"popers'tsi,"* breastplate. All this is more
      likely than the "translation" *"zhelezni̇e parobtsi,"* iron
      fellows, concocted recently by patriotic scholarship
      (Orlov, followed by Lihachyov).

555   Hin: see note to 437; Yatvangians: *yatvyazi*, a
      Lithuanian tribe; Dermners: *deremela*, probably
      another Lithuanian tribe, also known as Dermen or
      Dermne.

567-570   This unexpected statement has been variously
          explained: "The Don (which, you claimed, called
          you) is still calling you and the other princes. You,
          the descendants of Oleg Malglory, have been too
          hasty in waging your war." But all this is guesswork;
          and there exist some even less convincing glosses.

line

571-583   Ingvar and Vsevolod, two Volhynian princes active
in Igor's time, sons of Yaroslav of Lutsk (House of
Mstislav) and brothers of Mstislav of Peresopnits
mentioned at 542; and the three sons of Mstislav of
Smolensk (d. 1180), son of Rostislav I: these, not
named in The Song, were: David (not to be confused
with his uncle, David of Smolensk), Vladimir, and
yet another Mstislav. The epithet "six-winged"
remains as obscure as the exploits of these three
young warriors.

584   The epithet "silvery" applied to "streams" (here, in
the archaic sense of "shafts of water") has seemed to
some commentators to be the odd foreglimpse of
a modern cliché. Cf. "Fragments" (p. 395, vol. II,
Laing's edition of *The Poems of Ossian*): "Blood tinged
the silvery stream."

591-610   Izyaslav (died in the Battle of Gorodets, 1162), son
of Vasilko and great-grandson of Vseslav (House of
Polotsk); and his two brothers Bryachislav of
Vitebsk, and Vsevolod (or "Volodsha").

595   It is here that for the first time falls the wizard
shadow of Prince Vseslav who will be the subject of
a special section.

600   The passage is garbled and obscure.

601   The attribution of this quoted phrase to Boyan is a
tempting conjecture.

608-610   According to Russian traditional belief, the seat and
point of exit of the soul is the hollow of the throat above
the chest bone, the triangular dimple called *dushka*. The
dress a prince wore under his mantlet was fastened on the
chest by a system of loops and had, higher up, a round or
square gap at the front of the collar. This opening (which
the soul might conveniently use for its exit from the
throat) was adorned with gold braid and precious stones
forming a broad band called the *oplechie* or, as in our text,
ozherelie (which I have rendered as gorget). Today the latter word means only necklace. The image of the soul
dropping out like a pearl occurs in religious works as late
as the seventeenth century (e.g., Avvakum's "Letters").

617   Possibly, Yaroslav of Galich. For Vseslav here and at
627 see further.

631   See note to 59.

631-678   Vseslav of Polotsk (d. 1101), son of Bryachislav and
great-grandson of Vladimir I. This turbulent prince
was deemed a magician. Taking advantage of an
insurrection that knocked Izyaslav I (House of
Yaroslav) off the Kievan throne, Vseslav became its
holder for seven months in 1068. The year before he
had taken Novgorod (the great city north of Polotsk,
see Map) which traditionally belonged to the House
of Yaroslav. This was immediately followed by the
Battle of the Nemiga (a river in the Minsk region)
where the three sons of Yaroslav I routed him. Vseslav
was sung by his contemporary Boyan, from whom our
bard seems to have borrowed certain details.

line

643-644   *Obyesisya sin ye m'glye*, having enveloped himself in a blue mist. Cf. *Fingal*, Book II (p. 64, vol. I, Laing's edition): "The blue mist . . . hides the sons of Inis-fail," and *Temora*, Book VI (p. 185, vol. II, *op. cit.*): "He clothes, on hills, his wild gestures with mist," and Book VII (p. 208): "From the skirts of the evening mist, when it is rolled around me."

645-646   *Utr zhe vozzni [voznzi] strikusï.* I follow the conservative commentators who dimly discern in the nonce word *strikusï* a weapon or war engine. Leonard Magnus, in the notes to his English translation (1915, p. 110) suggests reading *utr zhe vyazni v tri kusï* (he tore his bonds into three pieces) which he finds more sensible than *utr zhe vazni s tri kusï* (he cast off his luck in three bites). Jakobson (in *La Geste du Prince Igor*, 1948, p. 196) substitutes "snatched" for "cast off." All this belongs to the category of linguistic parlor games.

648   Yaroslav I, founder of the House to which Vseslav's foes belonged.

650   From Dudutki: *s Dudutok*. This place name has never been exactly identified. Basing himself on unknown documents, Karamzin, 150 years ago, suggested that the reference is to a monastery at Dudutki, near Novgorod. The playful imagination of some commentators has dissected and recombined *s Dudutok* into various odds and ends of specious sense.

line

651-658   The bloody battle which Vseslav lost on the river
           Nemiga took place on March 3, 1067 (according to the
           Lavrentiev Chronicle). He was vanquished by the sons of
           Yaroslav I (Izyaslav, Svyatoslav and Vsevolod) and fled.

664   *Do Kur Tmutorokanya.* The capitalization of the sec-
           ond word (evidently a clerical error) induced the first
           editors to understand (instead of "cocks") "Kursk"!

665   Hors, the sun god (see note to 66).

666-670   This passage somehow always reminds me of the
           charming lines in Walter Scott's "The Last
           Minstrel," 1805, Canto Two, stanza XIII:

> In these far climes it was my lot
> To meet the wondrous Michael Scott,
> A wizard of such dreaded fame
> That when in Salamanca's cave
> Him listed his magic wand to wave
> The bells would ring in Notre Dame.

676-677   *Ni hitru, ni gorazdu, ni ptitsyu gorazdu* (neither the
           guileful, nor the skillful, nor the bird skillful). I fol-
           low Magnus (1915, p. 19 and p. 59) in amending the
           second line to *ni ptitsyu, ni gudtsyu.*

679   Our bard echoes Boyan with a prophecy of his own:
           Russia, too, cannot escape God's judgment.

682   Presumably, Vladimir I.

line

685   Rurik and David: See note to 511.

687   Lances hum on the Dunay: *Kopia poyut na Dunai.* I
       think the intonation here is the same as at 282-283,
       "What dins unto me, what rings unto me," and is, in
       a sense, the response to that melodious query.

688   Yaroslavna: this is Igor's second wife (since 1184),
       Euphrosyne, daughter of Yaroslav of Galich. She
       employs the name Dunay (specifically, the Danube)
       as a generic term for any great river (Magnus sug-
       gests, p. 69, that perhaps "Yaroslavna in her imagi-
       nation hears her father Yaroslav of Galich, preparing
       his men to relieve Igor"). It will be noticed that
       Euphrosyne has no tears for her stepson Vladimir,
       whose mother, Igor's first wife, died in 1183.

699-708 Cf. the apostrophe to the winds in "Darthula" (p. 381-3,
         vol. I, Laing's edition): "Where have ye been, ye south-
         ern winds! when the sons of my love were deceived? . . .
         O that ye had been rustling, in the sails of Nathos [son
         of Usnoth], . . . It was then Dar-thula [daughter of Colla]
         beheld thee, from the top of her mossy tower." And
         also Colma's complaint in "The Song of Selma" (pp.
         455-456, *op. cit.):* "Cease a little while, O wind! stream,
         be thou silent a while! let my voice be heard around. Let
         my wanderer hear me! Salgar! it is Colma who calls."

711   *O Dnepre slovutitsyu.* A folklore epithet with a homey
       intonation difficult to render in English. Some under-
       stand "son of Slovuta" son of renown, or identify
       Slovuta with a tributary in the Dnepr's upper reaches.

line

712-713   This refers to the rapids (*porogi*) just east of meridian 35°.

731   Here begins the last part of The Song. The forces of nature heed Euphrosyne's plea. One wonders if the "God" at 733 is not a pious transcriber's amendment for "Stribog."

738-739   *Igor spit, Igor bdit.* One moment he sleeps, he keeps vigil the next. The crisp rhyme and concise rhythm cannot be rendered.

741-742   Our bard sees his hero as being further to the east than the historical Igor was at his place of captivity.

     When did Igor escape? The Ipatiev Chronicle says that he remained "that year" (1185) in the Kuman camp. The Lavrentiev, on the other hand, says only: "*I po malih dney uskochi Igor*'" (And not many days later Igor escaped); but at least a year must have passed, and it is spring again, judging by the vernal phenomena depicted further.

751   The escape of the historical Igor must have occurred soon after he learned of Konchak's doings in the Pereyaslavl's region in the beginning of 1186 (see note to 494-496). It was rumored that upon Konchak's returning to the prairie all the princes would be put to death, and Igor, who had earlier refused to avail himself of a chance which the other captive princes had not been given, now decided to take it. According to the chronicle, he had a not too arduous time in captivity. He was allowed to go hunting with his hawks. He had a Russian priest

line

brought from the Kievan region. The chronicle also corroborates our bard's account of Igor's escape. He had sent word to Lavor (Ovlur, Vlur), a friendly Kuman, possibly a kinsman, to cross to the farther bank of the river Tor (a tributary of the Donets, see Map) with a led horse. The guards were drinking fermented mare's milk and making merry. Igor took advantage of this to join Lavor. The chronicle tells us that God rescued Igor on a Friday. After fording the Tor he rode off but apparently soon dismounted: the chronicle says, "He walked on foot eleven days to the town of Donets." From there he proceeded to Novgorod-Seversk. After that he traveled to Chernigov for a conference with Yaroslav. Finally he went to Kiev where he was welcomed by Svyatoslav III and the co-ruler Rurik.

757 *Bosim volkom*, as a werewolf. The adjective has also been explained as meaning "bare," "barefooted," "white-footed," with various connotations of survival, might, and magic (see also note to 407).

768 *Trusya soboyu studenuyu rosu*. This admirable image refers to the long damp grasses of the prairie in springtime.

778 *Ne malo ti velichiya:* Not small is unto thee the fame (the glory, the greatness). Cf. a similar intonation in *Fingal*, Book I (p. 18, vol. I, Laing's edition): "But small is the fame of Connal!"

line

783   The epithet has been explained by some as applying
       to the chalky coloration of the banks.

791-802   Rostislav of Pereyaslavl, son of Vsevolod I, brother
           of Vladimir Monomachus, and paternal ancestor of
           Igor's wife, was drowned in the Stugna (a tributary of
           the Dnepr, a few miles south of Kiev) in 1093, while
           attempting with his luckier brother to ford it during the
           retreat, following a disastrous affray with the Kumans.

796   *Rostre na kustu* and 799, *Dnyepr temnye berezye.* An
       obscure and corrupt passage, line 796 has been also
       understood as "she widened toward the issue" (*k
       ust'yu*), and 797-798, as "imprisoning him at the bot-
       tom near (*dnye pri*) the dark bank." The sudden
       appearance of yet another river, the great Dnepr, is of
       course stylistically rather disturbing; but the "*dnye pri*"
       is a most artificial combination which no poet could
       endure exactly because of the resemblance to that very
       "*Dnyepr*" which supposedly fooled the scribe.

814-830   The Ipatiev Chronicle contains a different dialogue
           conducted by the historical Konchak and Kza. The
           connection between it and the structural conversation
           composed by our bard is as evident as it is inexplica-
           ble. Here is the chronicler describing the somewhat
           chaotic plans of the Kuman leaders after their victory
           over Igor: "Quoth [*molvyashet*] Konchak: 'Let us
           march on the Kievan side where our brothers and
           our great prince Bonyak have been beaten.' And Kza
           quoth: 'Let us march toward the Seim where the

line

women and children have been left [in Putivl]: a collection of captives is ready for us; as to the town we shall take it without risk.'" Konchak attacked Pereyaslavl (see 472-476), and Kza Putivl, but neither managed to take those fortresses. Falling back, Konchak destroyed Rim, and Kza wrought havoc in the Seim region. It should be noted that the historical Kza (as well as the poetical Gza) seems more commonsensical and prudent than the vainglorious Konchak of history and art.

831-832   Song-maker of the times of old: *pyesnotvortsa starago vremeni.* Cf. "The War of Caros" (p. 235, vol. I, Laing's edition): "Bard of the times of old."

833-834   *Svyatoslavlya . . . , Yaroslavlya, Ol'gova, Koganya.* *"Kogan"* or *"kagan"* was a title given to Hazar and Avar chieftains and sometimes applied to the Russian princes of the XIth century. The princes sung by Boyan might have been Svyatoslav II and his sons Yaroslav and Oleg (see Pedigree).

831-834   The passage is very muddled in the text. This is the best I can do.

843-846   Artistically these maidens weaving their songs at a distant southwestern point on the Danube (unless this is the same generalized Dunay that Euphrosyne evokes) form a curious counterpart to those other maidens who perform on the shore of the blue sea at 444-449. It is conjectured that here, at 843-846, the reference

line

is to Russian colonies on the lower reaches of the Danube, but the roundabout way the songs take to attain Kiev remains rather odd.

847   This slope, several times mentioned in the chronicles, is located in Kiev.

848   This church was founded by Mstislav I in 1132, and is one of the very few Christian allusions in the poem.

856   According to the Ipatiev Chronicle, Vladimir son of Igor returned to Novgorod-Seversk, with wife and child, in the second part of September, 1187. The Christian rite of marriage was performed *post factum*, and his bride, Konchak's daughter, received (according to Tatishchev in his *History of Russia*) the baptismal name of Svoboda, Liberty. In The Song there is no indication to the effect that our bard completed it *after* Vladimir's return; but his "glory" to Vladimir implies that he knew of the young prince's being alive and married (according to Kuman rites) in the place of his not unpleasant captivity which he must have left sometime in the summer of 1187.

860   *Knyazem slava, a druzhinye Amin'*. As it stands, this ambiguous phrase rather pointedly dismisses the retinue with a curt amen while glorifying the princes. The line should probably read: "Glory to the princes and to the knights," with "Amen" appended by a pious transcriber. Or perhaps, the word *chest'*, honor, has been left out between "knights" and "Amen."